Dedicated to God's champion
TIMOTHY PAUL GARDNER

-RG

AGENT SAUL

ROBERT A. GARDNER

ARCHWAY
PUBLISHING

Unless otherwise cited, scripture taken from the King James Version of the Bible.

Scripture quotations marked (NIV) are taken from the Holy Bible, New
International Version®, NIV®. Copyright © 1973, 1978, 1984, 2011 by Biblica,
Inc.™ Used by permission of Zondervan. All rights reserved worldwide. www.
zondervan.com The "NIV" and "New International Version" are trademarks
registered in the United States Patent and Trademark Office by Biblica, Inc.

All hand drawings by Author-Robert Gardner

Archway Publishing books may be ordered through booksellers or by contacting:

Archway Publishing
1663 Liberty Drive
Bloomington, IN 47403
www.archwaypublishing.com
1 (888) 242-5904

Because of the dynamic nature of the Internet, any web addresses or
links contained in this book may have changed since publication and
may no longer be valid. The views expressed in this work are solely those
of the author and do not necessarily reflect the views of the publisher,
and the publisher hereby disclaims any responsibility for them.

Any people depicted in stock imagery provided by Getty Images are
models, and such images are being used for illustrative purposes only.
Certain stock imagery © Getty Images.

ISBN: 978-1-4808-7559-3 (sc)
ISBN: 978-1-4808-7560-9 (e)

Library of Congress Control Number: 2019902931

Print information available on the last page.

Archway Publishing rev. date: 03/25/2019

CONTENTS

CHAPTER ONE
AGENT SAUL

As always in summertime, the sultry, sweltering air of the Judean desert sucked the life out of Saul as he drove his Denali SUV through the streets of Old Town Jerusalem. He kept his head on a swivel and "stayed frosty," as soldiers often say in the military. He was always watchful for the death that lurked around every corner, whether in the shadowy, dark alleys of night or boldly in the brilliant daylight of a sidewalk café. Death, Saul knew, was everywhere; it was a stalker, a hunter.

After easing his foot off the accelerator, he slowed to a stop under the shade of an ancient Kermes oak.

The big Denali with tinted windows, thick bulletproof glass, armor plating, and black-rimmed tires was his trademark vehicle. The other trademark was the aviator sunglasses he wore. The silver-rimmed glasses hung easy on a perfect aquiline nose, gendered from royalty and high position. Hazel eyes stared through them with focus, vigilance, and lifeless caring about those he searched for and loathed.

On his forehead, rivulets of sweat glided down through a forest of ebony hair and past his rugged, tanned face with high cheekbones. The droplets disappeared into a short, groomed beard peppered with desert sand and streaks of gray.

Deep in thought, Saul sat and analyzed every passing face. His anticipation of his quarry drowned out the droning of the SUV's pulsating air-conditioning that toyed with the blistering heat and particles of dust that floated in the stifling air.

Waiting was always hard, but the prey was worth it. Those "Followers of the Way," those so-called Christians, never left his mind. They never ventured far from his daydreams or his nightmares.

Saul was no ordinary agent of Jewish Homeland Security (JHS). His clearance was beyond top secret, and no one dared question his methods, not even weary politicians from the Pharisee or Sadducee parties. Not even the Mossad, the Israeli secret service agency. Even the Roman authorities left him alone, partly because of his Roman citizenship but more because of his reputation. When the work was secretive and dirty, they all called Saul. He was their investigator and enforcer, the man of many secrets buried in torture, intimidation and above all results.

He believed in the Laws of Moses and the traditions of his people from boyhood. His whole life was a fierce education, honed with singular passion to be the best. Beyond the universities, beyond the disciplines of languages, science, math, and diplomacy, he excelled in the schools of special operations, counterterrorism, and unspoken ways of making people talk.

His target now, the one man who stole his mind by day and robbed his nights of sleep, the target who quickened his pulse and set loose the dragon of determination, was elusive and cautious. It was the local leader of the Followers.

Saul knew the growing heresy must end. He knew that he was close and could once and for all erase the Followers of the Way even as the Sanhedrin had pressured the Romans to crucify their fake messiah.

Saul's mind drifted off for a moment in the heat and glare of the noonday sun. He mentally unpackaged a recent case about the disappearance of a prominent socialite couple from the upscale Nicosia neighborhood, Ananias and his wife, Sapphira. They were reported missing by family members after a real estate deal went bad. Some thought they were murdered, others thought they were poisoned, and the crazies (and there was plenty of them lately) said they died of some hocus pocus supernatural stuff. *Just rumors*, he thought.

Saul's trained eye caught a stirring in the crowd. A lone, short figure in a white T-shirt, faded shorts, and well-worn sandals making his way cautiously toward the black SUV. The jostling market crowds, animals, and vendor carts swarming with hordes of flies did not hinder the messenger as he batted and pushed his way forward. Saul's network of spies and informants earned their pay or paid for it with their lives.

Breathing hard and sweating from every pore, the drenched, exhausted messenger stopped inches away from the Denali's driver window, never daring to touch it. Saul cracked the window but continued to stare forward, never looking directly at the man.

"Hefe," the messenger nervously said, taking quick looks right and left while trying to catch his breath. "I know the house where the Way Followers meet," he continued between gulps of air. "Their leader is a guy called Stephen."

The messenger finished his report with enough detail that Saul smiled ever so slightly. The intel was good. Saul didn't say anything; he lightly touched the gas pedal and drove off.

The drive back to the JHS headquarters took only a half-hour if it was not rush hour. The Denali passed the security checkpoints, entered protected grounds, and cruised toward the ramp that dropped steeply into the main underground parking area filled with agency cars. The SUV slid comfortably into its usual secure parking spot.

Saul sat there deep in thought. Without turning off the engine, he leaned over and switched on his console computer. He entered "Search" and then the name "Stephen," along with his middle and last name, "Mordecai Rosenberg". Within seconds, Stephen's face and stats filled the screen. Stephen's three-dimensional image floated in a green background with statistical data flashing next to it. Each time the face rotated forward, it seemed to stare back directly at Saul as if examining him.

"This guy doesn't look like a zealot," Paul muttered to himself. "His eyes are focused, but kind and subdued—not fierce, no angry glint." Saul continued to think and read the accompanying report. "Arrested, beaten, accused of lying, but no solid evidence … Caused a scuffle at the temple twice, claimed the dead Way leader, Jesus of Nazareth, was alive."

As Saul looked up from the computer and through the tinted glass, for the first time a strange stirring crept its way into his subconscious. He was one who never doubted. The certainty of his skills, his instincts, and his unquestioned talent for violence made him 100 percent sure about most things. But now this doubt, this strange sense of uneasiness, was uncomfortable. He wondered if indeed these heretics were not the people whom folks thought they were; disrupters, destroyers of the law, and blasphemers.

The thought was cut off. "No, no!" Saul shouted, pounding the steering wheel. He cursed over and over as if to frighten the intrusive and unwelcomed ponderings to leave his mind.

Collecting himself and with steeled rededication, he swore, "I will kill them all, every last one of them in Jerusalem, and every last one of them from here to Damascus! Every last one of them!"

The ranting was interrupted by the vibrating cell on the seat next to him. It startled Saul momentarily, but he recovered, grabbed it, and blurted a quick, "Yeah?"

The tinny voice on the other end reported, "Sir, we found him!"

Saul's eyes widened. "Go ahead. What else?"

"We're standing by waiting for your orders," the soldier continued. "I'll send you the location. And, sir, I'm sending you an e-report we got from our people at the Temple."

"Stay there. I'm on my way," Saul ordered before hanging up.

A few minutes passed before a high-pitched ding announcing the message's arrival. The e-report appeared on the console computer screen. Saul read intently as he lightly but nervously tapped the SUV's floorboard with his foot.

Some months earlier in a secluded part of Jerusalem's south district, twelve key leaders and a number of heretic followers of the Way met secretly. A mole agent hired by the Synagogue Libertines was able to get into the meeting. He reported that Stephen and six others were chosen to head up local recruitment and handle local business, including money. The leader of the twelve, a heretic named Simon Peter, said these guys were "honest, full of the Holy Ghost and wisdom." They especially liked Stephen because he was strong and not afraid of the Romans or us. The meeting broke up before we could get our strike team to the location.

As the report ended, Saul sat still for a moment and then slammed the gearshift into drive. The Denali answered immediately, backing up, turning, and then jolting forward with tires squealing and clawing at the asphalt parking floor first and then the garage ramp, bounding over speed bumps, zigzagging past concrete security barriers, and rushing onto the crowded avenue in front of JSH headquarters. The Denali's tires screamed vengeance as Saul slammed the gas pedal with increasing anger and at the same time exhilaration.

"We've got you now, heretic! We've got you now!" he growled through clenched teeth.

As the SUV accelerated, he leaned forward, fumbled, and finally pushed the white button on the dash that activated the console's wireless speakerphone. "Siri, call Extraction Team Alpha!"

The seductive female voice of Siri responded, "Calling."

A muffled sound of dialing, and then a sharp, "Alpha Team, Zero-One. Go!" The familiar voice that came over the speaker was Sergeant Meleck, Alpha Team's leader.

Saul replied, "Zero-Six here. Where is he now?"

Saul could hardly hear his Alpha Team sergeant's voice over

the roar of the powerful engine revving at near maximum RPMs. The SUV's big, fifteen-inch tires dodged right and then left, up and then down, hitting potholes and trash cans that had rolled into the narrow streets. He nearly ran over frightened people scurrying out of the way. Saul drove like a madman, relentless, possessed, and with only one thought: *End it today!*

The sergeant said, "Zero-Six, can you read me?"

"Go ahead, One," Saul replied as he eased his foot on the gas pedal.

"Sir, he's not hiding or running away!" Sergeant Meleck shouted. "He's standing in front of Claudius Caesar's fountain at the temple mall near the dress shops. There's a big crowd starting to gather." The sergeant cleared his dry throat and then continued. "He's saying stuff about Jewish history, calling the priests liars, murderers, stiff-necked, uncircumcised, and resisters of the Holy Ghost."

Saul interrupted. "What else did he say?"

Sergeant Meleck paused. "He said the whole Jewish Nations was responsible for killing Jesus of Nazareth, the Son of God!"

Saul let out a long curse and reapplied pressure to the pedal.

As Saul was about to sign off, the Sergeant's voice rose sharply, "Sir, wait a minute! The priest and a mob of bystanders with signs are throwing things and rushing the platform … They're beating Stephen!"

Saul slammed the steering wheel while violently twisting and turning the wheel to avoid hitting frightened pedestrians. "Send in your team, right now!" he ordered.

Static and sounds of distant shouting and gunfire came over the speakerphone.

Excited, Sergeant Meleck shouted in the microphone, "Sir, we've got him! He's bleeding, and his eye is swollen." There was static on the radio. While fading in and out, the sergeant continued. "They ripped his clothes like dogs attacking him, but he's still alive and … ranting some religious garbage." The young soldier's voice halted a split second. Then he said, "Stop! I said stop! Go back! I said go back!"

A few gunshots, then more shouting and more scuffling.

Saul listened to the melee and could feel his own heart racing. He remembered how quickly things could go bad when he was a young Defense Force enlistee.

"Sir," the soldier returned, "some of the priests and some other guys are following us. They want the prisoner! They're threatening to report the whole incident to the Forum."

Saul replied calmly but firmly, "Take him out back to the Johnson Creek field. Use the guarded south gate. Keep the reporters and whoever else doesn't need to be there away. Let's make this as quiet as possible." Then Saul added in code well understood by his men, "We don't want a lot of witnesses or another martyr. Got it?"

"Yes, sir!" Sergeant Meleck answered dutifully. "Zero-One out."

"Zero-Six out." Saul ended the call.

Twenty short minutes later, the SUV slid to a long, rumbling stop, momentarily hiding in a cloud of red dust and choking sand.

Through the dusty windshield, Saul saw the crowd holding tire irons, chains, sticks, bricks, and whatever else was lying around on the ground. He also saw his security squad protecting the prisoner. Saul pictured in his mind the frenzied mob, pulling and pushing in the dancing desert heat, resembling a swarm of feasting maggots and flies dressed in white robes and colored sashes.

Studying this eclectic crowd as he always did, by training and natural inclination, he noticed there were no sympathizers. He figured that the less unruly of the crowd from the shopping mall probably had dispersed under threats of being shot or arrested. The ones here—"The pure ones," he mused—were the ones at risk of public humiliation, the ones who would lose money and prestige: the priest and a few prominent citizens he knew had killing on their minds. But more important, Saul understood by complicity, they were here "to restore order and decency," like him.

As if on cue, the noisy mob hushed, stopped, and turned toward the black SUV. Saul opened the door and stepped out. The plain, black leather jacket filled with well-defined muscles; those big calloused hands; the wrinkled jeans; the bulge where he carried his two Glock 17s; and the sunglasses he wore so perfectly needed no introduction.

The crowd a few feet away from Saul parted in a half circle around the battered figure on the ground. Several Alpha Team members guarded Stephen and prevented the crowd from killing him before the arrival of Agent Saul. The once boisterous gathering of Jerusalem's finest stood uneasy but mute, not daring to say a word or move an inch.

Shadowing the man on the ground, Saul stepped close and squatted. He spoke with measured disdain. "So, you're the great Stephen Mordecai Rosenberg, huh?" It was less a question than the clear fact that Saul had finally caught his elusive prey.

Saul felt a thrill of delight when he saw Stephen cringe as he tried to lift his head. He watched as Stephen uncontrollably forced himself to his knees. Saul studied that swollen face, now almost unrecognizable, and the tears that slowly leaked from nearly closed eyes. He followed one single tear as it trailed the jagged path of preceding tears through dirt and dried blood, past bruised purple lips and free-falling onto dry soil that welcomed any moisture from rain, tears, or blood.

Stephen's quivering voice momentarily broke the trance that had overtaken Saul's thoughts. "Yes, I am." Staring into the hazel eyes of Saul, Stephen's voice gained strength. "Yes, I am Stephen, a servant of the Most High God, follower of His Son, my Lord Jesus Christ!"

Saul leaned back a little and glared but said nothing.

Stephen slowly lifted his head higher as if searching. All watched as his gaze became transfixed on something. He looked beyond Saul, past the angry men, as high as his trembling neck muscles would allow.

Saul wondered what the cloudless blue sky held for this unfortunate Follower about to die for nothing.

The crowd followed Stephen's gaze. "What's he looking at?" someone in the crowd asked no one particular.

Saul also gazed into the sky, and then slowly with studied intensity, he looked back at Stephen. He again wondered, *What hidden treasure deep within this man gives him the strength to stand to his feet, to be so defiant?*

Saul stood and backed away as Stephen cried out, "Lord Jesus, Lord Jesus … I see You!"

The murmurings of the acquisitive priests quieted for just a moment at the spectacle of Stephen, but the silence morphed abruptly into shrieks, cursing, and snarling.

Saul's attention also shifted back to the business at hand. The sudden, venomous transformation of the mob did not escape the imagination of Saul. They reminded him of the stories he'd once heard about demons possessing people, even the holy ones, like those gathered here.

"Officer Saul," a pious rabbi called, "let us kill him!"

Saul turned to the outspoken rabbi but gave no answer. He stared at him momentarily and then backed away, turning to give a nod to his security team to stand aside.

Saul walked back to his Denali. He hesitated to turn again and face the revolting maggots, but he did turn and stand silent and expressionless. He watched and listened to the rising crescendo of shouting, the gathering of stones, the clicking of illegal handguns, the twisting and rattling of chains, which raped the quiet field of peaceful Johnson Creek.

Saul guarded his feelings as he watched Stephen's gaze never leave the blue sky. To Saul, it seemed that Stephen was listening to something else, as if he seemed to hear none of the noise that would soon end his life.

For a brief moment, Saul remembered the ones whom he had

killed before Stephen. The women, men, and children. The "martyrs," they called themselves. The ones he imagined in the future who would also look up into the heavens and see what Stephen must have seen.

Through an opening in the frenzied mob, Saul saw Stephen once more and heard the chilling sound of death's agonal cry getting weaker.

"Lord Jesus, Lord Jesus, receive my spirit."

Saul saw Stephen raise his broken arms, still cuffed at the wrist, for the last time. He saw Stephen's lips move.

Saul leaned forward off the bumper of his Denali and strained to hear. *What's he muttering?* he asked himself.

Then Saul shivered as he heard, "Lord, please … lay not this sin to their charge."

Saul listened. The whispers turned to silence. Stephen moved no more.

The storm of hatred is finished. The ripping, cutting, and smashing of the heretic Stephen is done. The thirst for blood has been satisfied for this day. There will be more tomorrows and more setting things right, Saul thought to himself.

Strangely, Saul felt no relief, vindication, triumph, or solace. He didn't know what to feel.

He stood there with eyes close, allowing his senses to listen. He felt the cool desert wind of evening begin to blow gently. He felt the warm rays of the sun leave in its final descent to the west. Through the slits of his eyes, he could see the lengthening shadows of trees and rocks that stood witness to all that had happened this day. Finally, he sensed the night enveloping all and quietly bowing its head in sackcloth.

As the mob began to disperse and drift into the twilight, Saul took one last long look at the lifeless body of Stephen. His eyes settled on the seething mob of well-dressed citizens getting smaller as they lumbered back toward town.

Deep inside, Saul felt something strange, like feelings. He wasn't use to feelings about this kind of work. Feelings could get him killed. But something was shifting inside of him. He could not figure out if it was shame or rage toward those whom he served, or for that body lying still.

Turning toward his Denali, he opened the door and got back into the SUV. After pausing a moment to wipe the dust from his sunglasses, he felt something in the corner of his eye, a point of wetness that welled up from some unknown spring long hidden and forgotten inside of him—a spring that slowly became a tear, then a river.

CHAPTER TWO

NIGHT VISIONS

Saul sat behind a worn wooden desk in the poorly lit, smoke-filled squad room on the third floor of the JHS building. Deep in thought, he knew the Damascus raids had to be as perfect as the operations in Jerusalem.

The three-dimensional topographic map created by the agency's 3-D graphics section was invaluable in the planning of the next operation. It sat on a sturdy metal table next to him. The 3-D map was four feet wide by six feet long and was illuminated by a low-hanging florescent light suspended with chains anchored to the ceiling. Saul's tired eyes settled on the tiny spot where Jerusalem nestled among seven hills. On the map, the small green bumps representing Mounts Scopus, Olivet, the three peaks of Corruption, Ophel (the old Mt. Zion), the New Mt. Zion, and the hill on which the Antonia Fortress was built held his gaze. Then his eyes followed the long white line that went north into southwest Syria. It was the Damascus Highway. In years past, he remembered its name as the King's Highway, and it ended in Damascus, the city he again remembered from his childhood, which was called the City of Jasmine.

As he leaned closer, studying the map and muttering to himself, his plan began to take shape. He mumbled, "From Jerusalem to Damascus, 136 miles. That's about 5 hours by car." He continued his inspection of the map's relief features and terrain. "The landscape along the white line from Jerusalem swayed back and forth between … um … blistering daytime desert; tall, rugged mountains covered in trees and bushes of various heights; winding asphalt and dirt roads; and the blue lines of irrigated farmlands from the Bajada River."

Saul paused a moment to remember the training operations he had at night along that white line. He recalled the desert and how cold, dark, and unforgiving it was. He knew the danger awaiting those unfamiliar with its potential for natural death—and certainly death from unnatural causes like ambushes or snipers.

It was late, and finally his eyes could take no more planning. It was time to go home and get some shut-eye.

He didn't remember the drive home, only flicking on the light switch in his apartment. He removed his leather jacket and then the weight of his Glock 17s, slinging both across the back of a chair. Upon removing his shoes, he headed directly to the couch, lay down, and squeezed his eyelids, trying to force them to relax.

As the tension of the day slowly gave way to quiet, a face appeared in his mind's eye: Stephen. Saul opened his eyes in the darkness and then closed them, trying to rid those last imagines of Stephen staring at him and then into the sky. Then he saw the mangled corpse, sprawled grotesque and still. Saul turned on his side as if wrestling and hoping his change in position would change the movie that was running in his mind and stealing the sleep he needed so badly.

It was not a good change, turning on his side. Another, equally stressing movie began. It was Rebecca, his girlfriend. The movie continued with sound effects. There she was, standing in the doorway of his apartment. Outside, he could hear the thunder and lighting. The heavy rain, mixed with small flecks of ice, pounded against the apartment window. There she was, soaking wet from head to foot. Her long brown hair hung over her small shoulders like a weeping willow. Saul remembered her hair and how it smelled like roses when he gathered it into his hands and pressed it against his nose. The drenched curtain of brown now hung sadly, covering the silk collar of the blue blouse that clung seductively to her wet skin. Saul grimaced as the night camera panned to the sad expression pleading for understanding for what was to come next. He watched as she shivered and then took a deep breath of courage. He felt the coldness and tremors as she reached for his hand.

For a moment, he imagined why she was there. Their relationship had been strained by his elusive behavior, the secrets, his wanting to be alone to think, the incessant nights away without a word. He knew, and she expressed so many times, how she dreaded the phone ranging when he was away. He remembered holding her as she cried when he came home, and how the night exploded in ecstasy till the sun broke through the curtains.

Saul turned back over on his back, put his arm across his forehead, and stared at the ceiling. He saw a faint, shadowy glow from streetlights. For some reason, he felt tension rising in his right hand as he grabbed the couch fabric tightly and remembered more. The movie would not stop.

He imagined Rebecca looking into his soul, his fears and places in his heart that only she knew, places that would soften the words she was about to say.

"Sweetheart," I need to tell you something," Rebecca said while looking into his eyes.

Saul remembered the chill inside of himself. Those words, "I need to tell you something," were always bad news in Saul's world.

Then the bullet came. "Saul, I'm a Christian now." Rebecca released the words she'd held on to for so long.

Saul's mind refused to hear the words. He only remembered seeing her lips move.

"Becca, this is no time to be joking, honey." Saul remembered searching for clarity, hoping this was Rebecca just being playful.

His memory recorder played the dialogue that filled the dark apartment.

"I … I … wanted to tell you before, but …" Rebecca's voice trembled.

The darkness of the ceiling flashed bright as he clenched his teeth for the rage that followed in his mind.

For a split second in his nocturnal musings, he searched for penance to justify his reaction, which came as an errant bullet disguised as words. Nothing prepared himself for the thoughtless tirade he unleashed.

Saul heard himself scream, "Get out! Get out of here! Get out of Jerusalem! Never let me find you. Get out!"

The mental movie ended with Saul watching a terrified Rebecca back away, crying with hands to her mouth. She turned and raced out the open door and down the deserted hallway.

The credits rolled as the movie ended. There was only one credit, and Saul thought and then spoke quietly, "Me."

In the days that followed, Sergeant Meleck and others of Alpha Team noticed Saul's dark mood. His demands that the team shape up, try harder, and make no mistakes—this was not the leader who trusted them with his life.

Saul's rage on others was far less than the acrimony he inflicted on himself.

Rebecca's words, "I'm a Christian," pounded like a jackhammer.

"Why won't you leave me alone?" he'd yell to the walls of his apartment.

What was this power, this spell that attracts so many to the Nazarene? he pondered, staring into nowhere. *Why are so many willing to die for this nobody, Jesus?*

Saul reprimanded himself. "I've got to stop this madness! I've got to get my head on straight!"

Then as if in comic relief, a thought surprised even him. He pictured the believers as zombies in a horror movie. They were hapless creatures, infected and diseased, walking about dead but living.

He continued thinking and musing. "Yeah, zombies. Those heretics are dead zombies spreading disease of heresy and blasphemy." Saul reasoned to himself, "Believers are not human; they are just zombies, just animals."

With that, he forced himself back into his game face mode, his killing mode.

Saul was tired physically and mentally of the brainstorm that clouded his self-confidence and the mission his country expected of him to fulfill. It was late, but he could not sleep.

Saul was unshaven, barefoot, and dressed in boxer shorts and a short-sleeve shirt as he stood on the balcony overlooking Jerusalem. *It sparkles like diamonds,* he thought. Then looking up into the star-studded night sky, he wondered whether the God of Israel was still there.

He stood for a moment and then spoke as if to the audience of the universe. "I swear I will put a stake into the heart of every heretic zombie. I promise you, Father Abraham, this I will do!"

Though no response echoed from the dark heavens, Saul felt something seemingly press in all around him. A warm embrace of resolution and resolve that felt like an old friend. This strange sensation, though familiar, was at the same time different. It seemed to surround him and then stir within him, like something crawling from a hole in his stomach, slithering its way through his chest and finally curling with familiarity in his head.

The Feeling, he envisioned, sat on the throne of his conscience, erasing it clean of any guilt for the thing he was about to do to the Followers of the Way.

CHAPTER THREE

AMBUSH

Sergeant Meleck, Alpha Team's leader, and others noticed how Saul had changed since that incident with the heretic Stephen. He seemed quieter yet more determined, vicious, dangerous, and unpredictable then he had been during the hunt for Stephen.

Sergeant Meleck studied Saul as he made it clear at team briefings that he wanted every follower of the Way, whether man, woman, or child, erased from the earth, erased from history, erased from the minds of future generations.

To the sergeant, Saul had become obsessed, possessed, or whatever one called it; there was nothing else in life that mattered as he pushed and demanded more and more from the men in the unit. It seemed to Sergeant Meleck that there would be no relaxation or enjoyment for Saul with what few friends he had, or time to mend family ties he'd heard about, until the job was done in Damascus.

For nearly a year, the World News Network chronicled Jerusalem's relentless reign of terror. Some news critics in American and Europe decried the campaign as bordering on genocide and possibly crimes against humanity. Reporters from the *Jerusalem Gazette* leaked information from anonymous sources that special arrangements had been secured with High Priest Annas and Roman Governor Marcus Antonius Felix. The deal, the story continued, was based on "results."

In other words, the writer suggested, officials would look the other way when it came to Agent Saul and his assassins.

Other reporters, some who themselves had disappeared, produced photographic evidence showing the Followers of the Way, sometimes called Christians, being rounded up, beaten, tortured, imprisoned, or even executed without trial.

The stories began to decrease as pressure and intimidation from the JHS agents had its own effect on the media. What remaining information came mostly from hearsay—things like "There was no place to hide … large or small, rich or poor, every district, neighborhood, village, and mountain hideout was thoroughly swept by security teams."

Agent Saul demanded daily reports from his teams of Kill and Extraction Units (KEU). Intel was key, and his informants, including family members, disgruntled Jews, Greeks, and other weak Followers of the Way, along with JHS moles, were critical. He paid them handsomely or spared their lives, whichever got results.

It was time to go to Damascus. Saul's plan was to go by vehicle convoy. Not the well-recognized black SUV's but civilian, beat-up cars. Choppers would to be too noisy, and besides, the heretics also had their spies here.

Saul briefed his men. "Secrecy and speed are key. Damascus must not know we are coming."

Saul mused while leaning over the plans spread before him on the table. He pictured himself as the perfect storm filled with lightning, thunder, wind, and hail—and more important, death!

The convoy of ordinary vehicles eased out of an old, rundown garage on Nabius Road, near the Garden Tomb in West Jerusalem. The midmorning traffic was an excellent cover for the team.

Saul rode up front in the convoy of two cars and one minivan. The passenger side gave him time to think and observe. They blended in nicely and moved unnoticed with the busy Jerusalem to Damascus traffic, heading north. Most of the planning had been done. The five-hour trip of four lanes to three and then two lanes gave them time to go over the details. The mountain vistas were breathtaking with rich green valleys, small winding streams, orchards, and well-kept farms—all of which were hardly noticed by the team of assassins. As the trio of vehicles neared Damascus the traffic thinned of cars, replaced by animals pulling carts and travelers on foot, some with their thumbs out looking for a ride. The seriousness that never left Saul's face now became his game face, the expression that meant business. It was the one nobody messed with.

Just as Saul turned to asked the driver a question, time stopped in a brilliant flash, and there was a deafening explosion of dirt, concussion waves, and heat. Thoughts of "Ambush! IED, roadside bomb!" smashed into Saul's mind. The vehicles flipped onto their sides. Saul's driver draped over the twisted steering wheel, unconscious. From the broken rear glass, Saul saw the others trapped in their vehicles holding their ears, coughing, and shielding their eyes.

Saul's ears rang with excruciating pain. Powdery dirt filled his eyes, and he fought to clear them, but no matter how much he clawed at his eyes and face, he saw no light. He was blind! The thunderous explosive sounds continued to amplify even after the initial blast.

Then the voice. "Saul, Saul, why are you persecuting Me?"

Saul, trapped in his seat belt, jolted right and then left searching for the heretic, reaching for his Glock 17. "Who are you?" he demanded. Sensing all that was happening was not normal, he again asked, "Who are You, Lord?"

The voice replied, "I am Jesus, the one you're persecuting. You've been beating your head against a wall, trying to clear your conscience and wash your hands of the blood of Stephen, taking your anger out on My people."

Saul trembled, searching for the direction of the voice that was all around him and in him and everywhere! He asked weakly, after realizing it was no human that accused him, "Lord, what do You want me to do?"

Jesus answered him firmly, as one with authority, "Get up. Get up! I have appeared to you for this purpose: to make you a minister and a witness both of what happened here today and wondrous things that I will show you when I come to you again. I will send you to the Gentiles to open their eyes and turn them from darkness to light and away from the power of Satan. You will tell them their sins can be forgiven through faith in Me."

Jesus commanded, "Now, get up and go into Damascus, and someone will meet you there and give you further instructions."[1]

"Sir, sir ... are you okay?" Sergeant Meleck said as he tapped on the front windshield.

Saul's head snapped toward Sergeant Meleck.

"What was that voice and light, sir?" Sergeant Meleck asked breathlessly.

Saul, still shaking, struggled to free himself. "I can't see. I'm blind!"

Saul's men quickly recovered their training and drew weapons: Uzi submachine guns, M-79 grenade launchers, and the team's M249 light machine gun. They set up a defensive perimeter.

Sergeant Meleck looked over his shoulder to check his team's deployment. The men turned to watch their leader crawl through the broken side window.

Sergeant Meleck, adrenalin still high and heart racing, had sweat streaming down his dusted face. He tried to shake off the idea that something strange or even supernatural had just happened.

---

[1] Based on Acts 26:16–18.

CHAPTER FOUR

PAUL

It was dark by the time Saul's men drove him into the western suburbs of Damascus. They had confiscated a bread truck and a sedan to complete their journey. The back alley neighborhood reeked of rotting garbage, rats, barking dogs, and the ever-present homeless riffraff and druggies. The mission, needless to say, was on hold for now.

"Sir," Sergeant Meleck said, "I know this guy named Judas who has a small apartment over on Straight Street. It's one of our safe houses. He'll keep his mouth shut for a Benjamin ($100)." While looking at his haggard commander, Sergeant Meleck continued. "You can rest there until we figure out what to do next. I'll let headquarters know what happened. Should I tell them it was an ambush?"

"No," Saul said wearily. "Just tell HQ we're in a holding status."

Sergeant Meleck responded, "Okay, boss. I'll post a man on the roof across the street with a radio in case anything goes down."

Saul nodded and tugged at the blindfold protecting his eyes. "Tell anyone, just leave me alone," he added.

Sergeant Meleck snapped his response. "Yes, sir."

For three days, Saul didn't sleep, eat, or drink anything. He sat in the darkness of his mind. His eyes still felt like fire had gouged two holes in his face. Over and over, he interrogated himself, questioning whether all this was just a bad dream, a torment of a guilty conscious, or the prelude to insanity.

Each day the motel manager, Judas, offered him some food, water, pizza, or cold beer, but Saul refused. "Just leave me alone, I said!" He waved the manager away.

On the third day, Saul's politeness vanished.

While sitting on the bed, he grabbed his Glock 17 lying next to him—the one he had been cradling in his hand. With just a squeeze, he could end it all. He quickly raised the Glock and with a shaky hand pointed it toward the manager's voice. He bellowed, "Listen, you jerk, I said leave me alone! Get out and don't come in again!"

The motel manager got the point and eased the door shut.

Half sitting on the edge of the bed, Saul slid from the ragged, urine-soaked mattress onto the floor, the Glock falling from his hand. Saul found himself on his knees.

"Father Abraham, what have I done? All those people I hurt?"

In the moments that followed, Saul listened on his knees and elbows, but neither Abraham, the walls, the broken-down couch, the single wooden chair, nor the wilted jar of flowers on the coffee table answered him. Nothing near spoke to him. But outside, the disgusting things called: the distant bickering of drunks in the alley, the scurry of foraging rats in the dumpster, and the incessant hum of a transformer outside his window. The sounds of night filtered in. They too gave no solace to his inner darkness, the demons of his own making.

Then the mind movies started. Apparitions of hundreds whom he had imprisoned faded in and out of memory's shadows. The "maggot" priests and Jerusalem's finest citizens gloating. The tortured yet peaceful look of Stephen. The agonizing cry, "Lord, lay not this sin to their charge," echoed and reverberated until there was no place for the pressure of guilt to go but out.

Saul raised his arms into his dark skies just as Stephen raised his in the blue sky, and he cried piercingly, "See me, Lord! See me. Please see me!" Then he fell forward again and sobbed uncontrollably, pounding his fist over and over into the hardwood floor.

"Have mercy on me, Lord! Have mercy on this son of Abraham! This fool who didn't know who You were!" he moaned.

More sobbing, more pounding, more pleads for forgiveness.

Then the words Jesus longed to hear: "Lord, I ... I surrender to You."

Ananias, a secret follower of the Way, lived a half mile from the motel where Saul was hiding out.

Ananias did not consider himself poor, though he knew he was. Yet on quiet mornings just as the sun barely broke the sky and most folks were still sleeping, he'd sit on his front steps and ponder the day before him. Each morning, he thought how rich he was in blessings since he'd heard and believed the words spoken to him by the one called Jesus of Nazareth.

He remembered the sound of that soft, soothing voice of Jesus speaking to crowds on the hillside near the Sea of Galilee. He remembered the crushing newscast of His death, then the wonderful reports that He had risen from the dead. How he'd danced and spun around, praising God, singing, and running through the streets of Damascus shouting, "He's alive, He's alive, He's alive!"

The sun rose higher with gracious ease, turning the morning clouds into a dazzling color display of fuchsia and shades of gray. It reminded Ananias of a jeweled tiara. A contended smile spread across his face with a feeling of joy that he indeed was blessed.

Throughout his busy day, he often thought of himself as a simple man of little importance to any who saw him tinkering with his lawn mower though he owned no grass, fixing a neighbor's washing machine, or teetering on a roof adjusting satellite dishes. He felt good that he was useful and was the neighborhood's handyman.

Since retiring from his job at the auto plant, he was more laid-back about most things. He lived well on a small pension, he didn't have to shave, he ate well, and if he didn't have too much sour dough rolls and spaghetti with spicy oregano garlic sauce, he slept well. But despite the gastric summons that disappeared with acrimonious nocturnal vapors, he eventually drifted into a deep sleep. On those nights when his sleep was especially enjoyable, the next morning his neighbors reported to him. With caustic replies, they'd tell of his monstrous snoring causing them to stay awake, banging on ceilings, hammering on his door, shouting from apartments across the alley, flinging small stones and cans at his window, or unsuccessfully calling the police with complaints of noise disturbance.

Those mornings while standing in his striped pajamas, he would look at them from his front steps, stretch, and give a broad smile from his round, unshaven, happy face. They in turn would give a few boos, but eventually, out of love for this simple little man, they would smile back, throw up their collective hands, and return to what they were doing. Despite his quirkiness and occasional sleep-robbing habits, they knew he was honest, hardworking, generous, and a man who loved God.

That third night Saul wrestled with his demons, Ananias was

across town. He stirred fitfully in his sleep. An annoying light poured through sleepy eyelids.

"It can't be morning already," he grumbled to himself.

Suddenly it was as if he had no eyelids. The whole room filled with a shimmering light of alternating gold and silver. Then a voice called: "Ananias."

He bolted upright in bed and squinted through his fingers covering his eyes.

The whole room pulsated with a warm, gentle light. Then the voice again. "Ananias, wake up!"

He recognized that voice. It was the one he'd heard in Galilee. Ananias answered, "I am here, Lord. Your servant waits."

The Lord said, "You are a faithful servant, Ananias. I want you to get your clothes on and go to the Judas Motel on Straight Street."

Ananias listened and hesitated to speak.

The voice continued. "There's a man there from Tarsus. He is praying. I know his heart."

"What's his name, Lord?" Ananias bravely queried.

"Saul," the Lord answered.

Ananias's heart almost bulged through his nightgown, nearly stopping.

"Saul? Agent Saul?" he blurted. He wheezed and for a moment felt dizzy. Breathlessly he continued. "I've heard of the terror and death he has caused to the believers in Jerusalem. He's backed by the Temple thugs and the Romans!"

The intensity of the light brightened momentarily with some irritation and then went back to softness.

The Lord, mindful that His servant was indeed a simple man, assured him, "That's not your problem. Saul is My chosen vessel. I have groomed him to carry My name to the Gentiles, to kings, and to the children of Israel this day and for generations to come."

The Lord continued. "Tell him that which the Lord ask will not be easy. Tell him I have chosen him and will be with him."

Ananias was thinking of asking more question when the Lord intercepted his hesitation with, "Now, go!"

Ananias dressed quickly, unchained his rusted bicycle from the telephone pole next to his house, adjusted the seat, took a deep breath, and then made his way to Straight Street.

The streets were still. Morning traffic had not started yet. A few cars passed him narrowly, and a huge, rumbling street sweeper almost got lucky and hit him.

Undaunted, Ananias peddled briskly, dodging potholes and swatting hungry mosquitoes. As he gripped the handlebars, he imagined himself tearing down a racetrack on a sleek, shiny motorcycle. With cheeks puffed and lips pursed he imitated the raucous sounds of a Harley Davidson.

Finally there it was, the Judas Motel, advertising vacancy in broken red and blue neon lights. In front of the door was a faded straw welcome mat littered with years of chewing gum and cigarette butts. Along the sides of the building lay a landscape of old newspapers, boxes, discarded needles, and broken crack pipes. Vagrants or perhaps teens with time on their hands spray-painted gang slogans, profanity, and obscene pictures, which were partially covered with pasted leaflets for rent notices or missing dogs or cats.

Ananias got off his bike and carried it up the short cement steps to the front door with him. He dared not leave it outside. He pushed the manager's button repeatedly before noticing it was cracked and obviously hadn't worked in a long time. He then started pounding on the thick wired glass of the door until a bent-over, beady-eyed man inched the door open.

"Yeah, what do you want?" the man snarled.

"Where is he?" Ananias asked the manager.

Without much conversation, Judas knew not to ask too many questions, but he reasoned, *This guy must be with those other guys from the other night.* Judas looked past Ananias, up and down the near deserted street, and then at Ananias and his bicycle. "Come in." He closed the door behind them. "Leave your bike here." Judas pointed to the side of the sign-in desk. Then he turned to a window facing the street. "The guy down the hall said he didn't want any visitors." Directing Ananias gaze out the window and across the street, he said, "See that guy on the roof? See the scope on his rifle? He's looking at you right now, so be careful what you say and do. Got it?"

"Yeah," Ananias nodded.

The manager said, "He's down at number three." Turning into his own room, he added, "Remember—I never told you nothin'. Got it?"

Ananias cautiously walked over creaking floorboards and down a hallway with one forty-watt light bulb swinging on a frayed wire. He pinched his nose to stifle the smell of urine that hung heavy in the air.

"Number three ... ah, here it is," he whispered to himself. He tapped softly, hoping nobody was home. He tapped slightly harder one more time before considering leaving.

Somewhere in the back of his mind, he thought he heard a voice: "I'm watching you."

But then another voice sounded from number three.

"Go away. Please, go away," a muffled voice, weak and pitiful, called through the door.

Ananias cleared his throat, "Mr. Saul, the Lord sent me."

Silence.

Ananias spoke as evenly as he could, trying to dampen the fear in his voice. "The Lord sent me here to ... to talk with you."

Silence.

Then the flaking painted door creaked open slowly. The two faced each other, one quiet, exhausted, disheveled, and dejected and the other simply disheveled because that was how he dressed.

Ananias entered the room nervously. He quickly took in the filth, odor, and chaos of the apartment. He walked in while Saul closed the door. Turning toward Saul, he steeled himself to give the

Lord's message. With hesitation but gentleness, he took Saul's arm and led him back toward the bed while he pulled the wooden chair close.

"Brother Saul, the Lord, even Jesus who appeared to you on the Damascus road, has sent me here to give you a message." He paused a moment. "While I was cycling here, He told me that once you heard His message, He would return to you your sight."

Saul started sobbing again, clutching his knees, and opening and closing his fists in anguish.

Ananias continued. "You are greatly loved by Him. You are His chosen one. He has heard your prayers." Ananias's fear left him, and he felt a great compassion for Saul. He placed one hand on Saul's shoulder, took a deep breath, and with eyes closed placed the other hand on Saul's head.

Ananias prayed, "In the name of our Lord and Savior, Jesus Christ, He gives you the Holy Ghost."

Immediately, light flashed through Saul's matted eyelashes, down through darkened optic pathways, around nerve centers of anger and pride, and onward, speeding to neurons electrified by hope and joy and then exploding outward through quivering lips of gratitude.

"I can see! I can see! Praise God, I can see!" Saul shouted, jumping to his feet and then falling to his knees, weeping and sobbing this time for joy.

Before long, sunlight poured through the draped window. Saul ran to the window, tore down the ragged drapes, flung open the window, and shouted, "Praise God! I can see!"

Later that day, Saul ate some food and began to feel stronger. Although he no longer had twenty-twenty vision, he rivaled with inexpressible joy that he could again see. But he was even more joyous that spiritual blindness was also gone. For the first time in his life, as a son of Abraham, he felt the assurance that his sins had been forgiven.

As the evening sun disappeared behind the mountain shadows of Damascus in the west, Ananias and Saul quietly made their way out the rear of the motel and down dark allies, avoiding the streets as much as possible. Ananias offered Saul a ride on the handlebars of his bicycle, but Saul declined. Still wearing his sunglasses and black leather jacket, he simply said, "Thanks, but that's not cool. I'll walk."

From that time on, Ananias could hardly contain himself as he introduced his new brother in Christ, Saul. They spent many hours each day, which morphed well into the nights, talking about Jesus and the Holy Spirit gift He'd left to His followers.

Not all the believers in Damascus were enamored by Saul or believed he had changed. Many felt it was a JHS trick or scheme to draw them out and kill them.

After nearly a week of being missing and the unpleasant interrogation of the motel manager, Saul's men found him at Ananias's house. Sergeant Meleck stood on the steps in front of Ananias house and asked to speak with Saul alone.

Ananias watched as the two walked into a back room. He could hear low voices, and after a few minutes, he heard the sergeant say, "I'm sorry, sir." Then in a sad but professional tone, he added, "I'll report your decision to HQ. Good luck, sir."

Sergeant Meleck walked past Ananias and into a waiting black SUV that had no inscriptions or logos.

Saul emerged quietly from the back room and stood in the doorway.

Through the dark window glass of the vehicle, Sergeant Meleck took one last look at his commander and friend standing in the doorway. He wiped his eyes as though tired and secretly smiled.

The heavily armed men in black SWAT uniforms drove off in their SUVs.

Saul watched the trail of dust from the departing Alpha Team disappear into a cloud mingled with ghostly images of market vendors, animals, trucks, and cars going about the ordinary things of life.

He stood there a long time, staring at nothing. His mind flooded with memories good and bad. Many things had changed, but he knew deep in his heart he would miss his men and especially his friend, Sergeant Meleck.

In the days and weeks that followed, Saul spent many wonderful hours speaking, teaching, preaching, and praising God to the amazed believers and nonbelievers in Damascus. His newfound faith and boldness took him to the Jewish synagogues, where some who heard him were astonished. Others publicly challenged him with, "Isn't he the agent who raised havoc in Jerusalem among those who called on the name of Jesus?" The uproar from other doubters declared, "He has come here to take us prisoners in handcuffs to the Chief Priest and Roman dogs!" The naysayers did not dampen the enthusiasm of Saul.

Saul preached with power from the Holy Scriptures day after day, proving that Jesus of Nazareth was the Messiah, the long-awaited promise and gift from God to Israel. But even more surprising and controversial was the claim that God now offered the same promises and gifts to Gentiles and all who would believe. He was on fire in his new faith. He was born again, and before long he realized he needed a new name. A name not synonymous with fear and intimidation. An ordinary name. His new friends called him Paul of Tarsus. From that time on, Agent Saul was dead.

CHAPTER FIVE
ANTIOCH

Agent Saul, now disciple Paul, had no idea the journey of faith, powered by his forgiveness, that he was about to undertake. His miraculous conversion to Christianity was met with supsicion, lingering fear, and cautious jubilation among belivers. Rumors of supernatural happenings among the Way Followers also gendered intense hatred, talk of treason, and vendettas from other Jewish Homeland Security agents.

The work of Paul was tireless and passion driven. It resulted in unbelievable progress and growth among followers of the Way. Paul traveled by land, sea, and air though Middle East countries like Egypt, Lebanon, Syria, and Turkey, and those around the Mediteranian Sea (like Crete, Italy, Sicily, Cyprus, and Greece). He went every place where Jews and Gentiles needed to hear about the one they called Jesus.

Paul hated flying in modern jet aircraft, or even the propeller ones, for two reasons: height and cost of tickets. He often drove, went by ship, took a motorcycle, or hitchhiked.

Many churches and Christian friendship clubs were organized along the way. Needless to say, among believers, especially the young, he was a rock star, but among nonbelievers he was more a public nusiance and threat to Jewish tradition and Roman law.

The city of Lystra, Turkey, was located in the southeastern area called Anatollia. It was part of the Roman province of Galatia and was where the Romans built a modern, four-lane highway dotted by service stations, bike paths, and rest stops linking Lystra to Iconium in the north.

Paul had trouble in Iconium.

But fortunately before Iconium, Paul met a man named Barnabas. This faithful local church leader was commissioned by the Jerusalem church to find someone to help with the work in the commercial cities and smaller towns, including Antioch.

The enormity of the task was not lost on Barnabas, or the fact that he needed help in organizing the fast-growing body of believers.

As Barnabas sat in his basement apartment, only one man came to mind, a man who lived in Tarsus: Paul.

Thanks to the Internet, plus a little good fortunate, Barnabas sent a text message to a friend, who texted a friend, who knew a guy who worked with another guy, who got the message to Paul. The invitation was accepted.

After meeting for the first time, the two became instant friends and coworkers; each with his unique skills that God blended for the special work among the Gentiles.

Barnabas, like most people, had heard or seen news articles about the infamous Agent Saul, but he had also heard through the Middle East grapevine how Agent Saul had given his heart to the Lord Jesus and had received a nod of approval from the Twelve Apostles in Jerusalem.

The two were not always about business; there were times when they just had fun hanging out together. Barnabas, or Barn as Paul playfully cajoled him, had his lighter side. Barn would laugh it off and then come back with the rock star title that made Paul cringe, but then they'd both get teary-eyed and laugh uncontrollably, snorting like teenagers and holding their stomachs. They were best friends forever and shared good times and bad times.

Barnabas was an inch or two shorter then Paul. His curly light brown hair sat upon a round face that was always smiling. He was broad shouldered, and his big, calloused hands told of a life of hard work and persistence. His round belly also spoke of junk food and a few extra delicacies. But what caught people's attention, especially Paul's, was his happy face. Above each eye was perched eyebrows the color of his hair, but they could be oddly mistaken for taxidermed caterpillars neatly tacked to his forehead. His rather full earlobes playfully peeked through the curls of thick sideburns. When all was said and done, he was likeable, charming, and a powerful preacher.

Antioch was a major city of south central Turkey. It was situated near the mouth of the Orontes River, about twelve miles northwest of the Syrian border.

Tourist brochures and Dark Web news described it in their own unique ways. For one, it was the sum of every city where neon lights never went out. It boasted of luxury hotels, overpriced condos, and sprawling high-end malls with addresses like Valentinos, Versace, Sacs, and Louise Vuitton. Yes, there was even a Super Wal-Mart for the less wealthy. However, from the other came stories of salacious gentlemen clubs, cheap strip joints, casinos, nude spas, and places too dangeous to be in after dark.

The tourish brochures would carry the prospective visitors or investors away from the beehive of vice and decadence to palm tree–lined streets, decorative million-dollar homes with half-acre Infinity swimming pools, manicured lawns with ornamental drive-ways embellished with statues of patron gods, and hanging gardens glimmering with every known species of roses, orchids, and the ordinaries that added color and alluring fragrances to the air.

Amazingly, of all places of such unsavory reputation, the Gospel message was readily accepted with unexpected joy. And as a result, the once small band of faithful believers grew daily into hundreds of followers.

Whether embellished reviews of the tourist brochure or seedy Dark Web news, those who lived in Antioch knew the real face behind the façade of happiness that many pretended in Antioch.

Paul sensed the burden of sin resting on the people. He saw in their eyes the weight of a thousand guilty serects, the emptiness of wasted lives, and the kind of loneliness that filled the room when the music stopped, the laughter faded, and friends went home.

From his own life, Paul remembered the emptiness that made money feel like ash in one's hand, fragile, vaporous, and worthless. The empty torment of lives consumed with drug cocktails of uppers and downers. The venomous bite of alcohol. The demasculating orgies in secluded groves of immorality, and more, aways ending in embrassement and loss of some part of the soul.

While standing on a street corner and watching the people whom he would preach to, Paul thought to himself, *This place is truly alive, but without a heart.*

He pictured them jostling shoulder to shoulder every day, so close yet so far away from each other. Properous, but hopeless.

They need the good news of the Gospel, he thought. Then he spoke softly to himself. "And I will give them this news."

So it was that from street corners to auditoriums, Paul and Barnabas preached their hearts out, presenting the Lord Jesus in all of His magnificent glory. Paul quoted the words of Jesus the city needed to hear.

"Come to me, all you who are weary and burdened, and I will give you rest. Take my yoke upon you and learn of me, for I am gentle and humble in heart, and you will find rest for you souls. For my yoke is easy and my burden is light" (Matthew 11:28–30 NIV).

Hundreds responded and joined the growing church. The Holy Spirit blessed and energized the work at Antioch. The city would never be the same again.

Iconium, their next mission assignment, was trouble.

Upon leaving Antioch, the two evangelist made their way to Inconium. The first point of contact, like most places they went to, began at the synagogue, the seat of local Judaism.

Paul was a Jew. He loved his people and its traditions. His heart was always toward the sons and daughters of Abraham.

After removing his sunglasses and leather jacket, Paul would turn to Barnabas and say, "By God's grace, let's do this!"

Barnabas stuggled to remove his size-too-small Member's Only windbreaker, turned to Paul, and gave a thumbs-up. "Amen to that!"

The two waded through the crowds to the front. Each took a microphone, bowed their heads briefly, and then through the influence of the Holy Spirit lifted up the long-awaited Messiah.

Paul's eloquent voice was free of the threats and venom from his JHS years. Now it captivated his listeners with the mavelous wonders of Jewish history, the faithful patriarchs, the gift of God to the human family, His beloved son, the rejection by His people, His death and resurrection, and the promise of His return to make all things new. Then Paul would deliver the most powerful part of his sermons: his personal testimony of what the Lord Jesus had done for him on the Damascus highway.

The synagogue would erupt in praises to Yaweh and equal boos of blasphemy and sacrilege. Both rose like steam and ash from a volcano heaving to life.

The controversy and prejudices, conversions and divisions, continued for months throughout the city. Newspaper headlines heralded a divided city: "Out-of-towners Speaking Boldly, Infuriate Some, Win Some."

The turmoil was not like the political fights between democrats and republicans in America, or even between feuding governments. This was worse—pure hatred and evil surmising between religious people, Jews and Gentiles, both claiming God's favor for their side.

Local spies, moles, and priests kept the JHS office informed of the activities of the former agent, Saul.

Miles far away at the JHS headquarters, the usually quiet corner office with scenic views overlooking downtown Jerusalem, was the office of the director.

This day, the quiet serenity and vistas ended as the secure red phone with the white bulb began flashing. The ringer was turned off, but when turned on it would thump out the American song "Another One Bites the Dust."

The director, seated in his leather chair, paused a moment and took one deliciously long drag on his Cuban cigar before reaching for the phone. He knew this call was trouble and meant something that needed to be done off the record. The Cuban stokie helped to relax him.

He put the phone to his ear and spoke evenly. "Director Allen."

He listened to the voice on the other end of the call.

"What do you want us to do?"

His hands began to sweat. He listened as he combed his fingers over an empty area of scalp where thick black hair once grow and waved like fields of wheat.

"You know, Agent Saul was one of ours …"

He listened as the High Priest in Iconia made his request.

There was a long silence before the director responded.

Director Allen, sighed, took a breath, and then whispered, "Okay, I'll clear it with the Roman commander in Iconium. Take care of Saul your way. Don't let this get back to us. Got it?"

"Yes, sir, and thanks!" the priest said, and then added, "I'll send this month's payment and some extra for your kind help."

The call ended.

For a moment, the director thought he heard a double-click on the phone line before returning the phone to its cradle. *Naw, that was probably nothing,* he reassured himself.

Director Allen was not happy with what he had just authorized. He knew Agent Saul well, liked him as a professional, and admired his deadly efficiency … but he also feared him. A chill coursed in his neck, thinking of the consequences if word got out that he had approved the kill contract. He knew once he unleashed the religious folks on the religious folks there would be blood—lot's of it.

Eunice, a Verizon phone operator who lived in the Lystra district south of Iconium, was about to take her lunch break when she noticed a number come up on her computer screen. It was an odd number that always blinked an amber light; it should have been either green or red like the other calls. Next to the amber light was an electronic warning: "No recordings. No listening. Secret."

Eunice, like many women whose low-paying jobs teetered on the brink of boredom, could not resist the challenge of the amber light that said no to her curosity.

Besides, she thought to herself, *I need a little excitement.*

She listened. "Take care of Saul your way. Got it."

She recognized the voice of the high priest due to hearing him conduct temple business over the phone many times, but she didn't know the other voice.

A frosty sensation raced down her delicate neck and across her bare shoulders. *I must tell Mother!*

Looking right and then left, she grabbed her sweater, punched her time card and then hurried from the Verizon call center to her apartment a few blocks away.

Lois was Eunice's mother. Eunice had asked her mother to move in with her to help take care of her son, Timothy. Eunice and Lois had become Christians. They had heard the things that Paul had preached about, read the newspapers and magazine articles, and once saw him at a rally. They believed the good news and were overjoyed!

Eunice, in quiet reflection, would often think, *How blessed I am to have Mom.* She remembered when she was a little girl Lois's stories of the coming Messiah and the dreams she had of that day when all things would be made new.

After arriving at her apartment, she bypassed the ungodly slow elevator, bounded up the stairs two or three at a time, fumbled her keys, and burst into the apartment.

Breathlessly, Eunice fast-talked all that she had heard. "Mom, what do we do?" She stood hands out-stretched in supplication, waiting for an answer from Lois.

Lois turned her back to Eunice and paced back and forth, her mind racing. Then she put a finger to her lips and whispered.

"We must tell no one else. We must warn brother Paul and brother Barnabas right away!"

And so they did.

Paul listened and thought briefly about his old boss, the director, and what he would do if he knew that Paul knew.

Paul smiled a little and mused, "Yeah, he got it right—if I were Agent Saul he'd be packing his stuff for the moon."

Paul turned to Lois and Eunice and hugged them tightly, praising God and thanking them. Paul and Barnabas also thanked the faithful brethren in Iconium for their hospitality.

As night enveloped the city, the two missionaries offered a prayer of thanksgiving and protection for the small church. They got into a car and headed south along the dark mountainous Roman highway to Lystra and Derbe in the area of Lyconia.

CHAPTER SIX

LEROY HUGHS

Paul sat in the front seat of the car as it crested a high point on the mountain road. He could see the twin towns of Lystra and Derbe in the distance. Seeing the sparkling lights dancing in the desert air like diamonds and the dark sky canopy absorbing the cities energy reminded him of Vegas, Reno, or the LA strip. These were the unashamed playground of the rich and famous that knew no limits or excess.

He once played there too—not as a reveler but as a hunter of those who broke the law of the Fathers.

His thoughts continued. *All those strangers sharing laughter, love, and needles, their home away from home … They are so decadent and superstitous. What happens there, stayed there, sometimes.*

The cool desert air waft across his face and he felt a deep sadness for the people. But, just as quickly he thought of the possibilities of hope he and Barnabas could bring. His thoughts brightened as he pictured a pure white lilly sitting atop the dark miasma of a putrid swamp. The beauty of that precious flower is indescibable. In those cities were those who like the lilly had a heart toward God, and who would hear and accept the cleansing message of the Gospel.

Morning was breaking as the car arrived at the outskirts of Lystra.

They thanked the driver and watched him drive back the way they came.

Paul and Barnbas walked to the edge of the street, put down their backpacks, and sat on a bus stop bench. They prayed and asked for guidance in what to do next. Their prayer ended, they both sensed their prayers had been answered.

Guided by the Holy Spirit, they would begin their work on the edges of town, away from the Jewish neighborhoods, to avoid the incendiary prejudice and persecution they knew would come.

As they mingled with folks in the neighborhoods they soon discovered there were no synagogues in Lystra despite the Jews having money and influence. According to the locals, the problem was not religious but politics. Powerful councilmen passed ordinances that blocked the building of any Jewish synagogue or mini-temples. To no avail the Jews petitioned and even bribed, but met no success.

Paul learned that the city council was made up of Jupiter and Mercury worshippers who held a majority of the seats and were clearly in control.

Barnabas, not as scholarly as Paul, asked, "What's with this god thing that's holding up the temple building stuff?"

Paul explained to Barnabas the issue. "To the Romans the deity was called Jupiter, and to the Greeks he was Zeus. Jupiter was the chief deity among all the pagan gods. He was the god of the sky and thunder, often portrayed with bolts of lighting and an eagle or a strong oak tree."

Barnabas listened intently as Paul continued.

"Jupiter's popularity was the bomb, dude." Paul pointed to a billboard near the bus stop. "Look, man. Everywhere, billboards, posters, and shops are filled with little statues that sparkled when you shake them. There were marbled public fountains of his likeness, and if you remember, even the markings on the Israel Air Defense planes have an image of Jupiter and eagles."

"Whoa, man," Barnabas responded. "That's deep."

Paul continued. "Let me tell you about Mercury. He was Jupiter's son and a major Roman god. He stood among the twelve gods within the Pantheon at Rome. The Greeks called him Hermes. He was worshipped as the patron god of financial gain, commerce, eloquence, and poetry."

A week or so later, after Paul and Barnabas met up with some believers who found them a room and took care of their meals, they saw a morning news program about them.

The news anchor read her teleprompter. "We have an ongoing and disturbing story we've been following about two strangers spreading talk of a god who was said to be the God of all gods, even Jupiter!"

The anchor paused and looked straight ahead, clearly uneasy about this sensitive story. She spoke to the nameless millions behind the teleprompter. "Every news outlet, the web, newspapers, and morning talk shows are riveted with this story. When will it end?" Her voice rose in pitch. "One of the two is reported to be an ex-JHS agent named Saul, and the other a street preacher named Barnabas."

Paul and Barnabas looked at each other and then back at the TV screen.

The reporter ended her report with, "The credibility of these two heretics are no better then the other quacks and fanatics who stand on our street corners spouting nonsense, asking for money with noisy tin cups and outstretched palms!"

The screen faded to a comnmercial.

Just outside one of Lystra's gated and fortressed enclaves of the wealthy, a few blocks to the east, was an area called Black Bottom. Here, one found the darker-skinned migrants from Africa and the poor of every color from every nation mingling and trying to survive. Poverty was the best of their conditions, whereas disease and ignorance born of hopelessness reigned supreme. Drugs like Meth, cocaine, alcohol, weed, and pills of limitless variety were the only pleasure some had and was their only future. Caring had long since died. Dying wasn't the worst, it was never being missed, never given value or purpose in life.

Like with so many, these were the musings of Leroy Hughs the Unfortunate, as he called himself. Leroy would say, pretending to be someone else, *I am important! I am somebody!* Then imagine his face, a different face, on a stranger who lived far away from here. It was his way of raising his own self-esteem in society. "A mind trick," he'd mutter to himself.

Leroy liked to lay back and look at clouds. He'd think, *Ain't it funny how clouds just appear? Like stopped in the sky. You stare at them, and they don't move. Stop looking for a few minutes, and they done moved.* He paused in his thoughts. *That's how my life is, a cloud.*

Leroy would close his eyes and remember the story of his life. The inside of his eyelids became a movie screen of dark memories. The images flickered to life. "You're nobody! You're just the bastard son of a crackhead!"

An imagine of his mother: "I shoulda flushed you down the toilet, you worthless cripple, and your daddy too!"

The kids at school circling him. "Look at the chocolate cripple!" Then the laughter, finger-pointing, and stones thrown at him.

Tears glid quietly from the corners of his eyes.

With the movie and self-pity ending, he'd grabbed his two well-worn cedar sticks with rubber tips and drag himself to his customary begging spot near the University of Lystra.

The two-block drag to John R Street and East Warren didn't seen far anymore after hundreds of times in the rain, sunshine, and snow.

Every day they were there, the familiar broken sidewalks, weed-cluttered lots littered with garbage and swams of flies, abandoned and burned-out buildings, crack needles, and the pungent smell of human excrement.

He saw it, but he stopped thinking about it, stopped feeling it, stopped smelling it long ago.

Leroy would say to himself, *Leroy, you only need to make it to your spot. Just today. Not tomorrow, just today.*

East Warren Street was busy as always with university traffic and students going back and forth. Paul and Barnabas were driving toward the university to catch the students at lunchtime for a Bible study. Paul liked the young people at the university.

He would tell Barnabas, "These kids are really cool. They're not like the elites, the so-called experts and professors."

"How's that?" Barnabas asked.

Paul looked at the cars and people and waved his hand. "They're not jaded by the mythologic professors and Jewish scholars. They're the millennials. They do things their way. If you don't connect or be straight with them, they tune you out big time."

"Yeah, you're right about that," Barnabas reponded. "You've got about thirty seconds to make sense before the headphones go on, texting starts, nacissistic selfies commence, and they're zoned out." He smiled.

"Hey, Barn, pull over. See that cripple?" Paul interrupted their talk.

"Yeah. What's up, Paul?" Banabas asked as he pulled to the lane next to the curve.

As Paul opened the passenger door, he removed his sunglasses. He walked slowly toward the cripple. His gentle brown eyes met Leroy's crusted, dark, weary eyes.

Immediately, compassion welled up in Paul's heart.

Quietly to himself, as if in conversation with an invisible presence, Paul said inaudibly, *Yes, Lord, I see him.*

Paul moved closer to the man lying at the edge of the sidewalk, with bent back pressing against bushes.

The old tomato can he held out stretched rattled the few coins he'd collected. His hands began to tremble more nervously.

Paul never took his eyes off Leroy.

In the street cars began to back up behind Barnabas, and a few honked their horns, cursed and went around. Others stopped to watch. A group of students watched too.

From one group of students, someone said, "Hey, isn't that the guy on TV? The one in the leather and aviators? Is he the one on the news?"

Paul stooped eye level with Leroy. He took in all of Leroy: the smell, the dirt, the rags he wore, and the tears—especially the tears, the only water to ever wash Leroy's scraggly face.

Paul reached for Leroy's crooked, arthritic hand holding the the can. His hands wrapped around Leroy's and the tin.

Leroy was no stranger to Paul. The night before, a bright being appeared to him. Paul could not remember if it was a vision or a dream.

"Paul, the Lord has sent me to tell you about a man who is greatly loved," the shining being said.

"Who is he?" Paul asked.

The being waved a hand, cutting the darkness of the room into images like a movie trailer. There in the hologram theater, Paul saw the life of Leroy.

He saw him curled and contorted in the cardboard box someone had given him. He saw the restless anxiousness chiseled on Leroy's face. The sleepless, cold nights Leroy spent looking skyward, past the starry treasures of the night, hoping beyond expectation that God would hear his prayers from crusted lips. Paul heard what God heard as Leroy prayed: the wish to see his Creator in peace, the joy of life, and the opportunity to help others with his few coins.

"Leroy," Paul gently said.

Leroy's eyes flashed. "How do you know my name?" he said.

"Your prayers have been heard, son of Abraham," Paul told him.

Leroy's lips trembled uncontrollably.

"Stand up, Leroy. Stand up and walk!" Paul commanded.

Paul released his hands from Leroy's.

Instantly the cedar stick he held in one hand fell from Leroy's grip, and he stood straight and tall.

Flies and waves of nameless odors circled Leroy, but to him they could have been angels singing and the expensive perfume from an alabaster box!

He shuddered, cried, jumped up and down, and flung himself into the arms of Paul, unloading the tears of twenty years of hopelessness.

Bystanders watched the passion play. Leroy's joy started an avalanche of tears among the sidewalk audience.

Some who walked or drove down John R and Warren Avenue

often saw Leroy and knew their nickels and dimes would make no lasting difference in his life.

But now, with the miracle of Leroy, the miracle they saw with their own eyes, the cry arose. "The gods have come down to us!"

Agile and quick fingers raced over cell phone keyboards, and cameras clicked. The news spread within minutes that these two strangers were "Jupiter and Mercury, come to earth in the likeness of men!"

CHAPTER SEVEN

GOOD NEWS, BAD DAY

"It was a good day" Barnabas said as he and Paul returned to their apartment.

Paul nodded. "Yeah, God is good."

After a short evening devotional, the two retired to bed.

Neither could sleep, however, because of the muffled noise of news programs blaring from TVs in apartments above, below, and next to them. Both eventually got up, and Barnabas turned on the TV.

Nearly every channel had stories of the day's event at the university.

"Tradition has it that the gods occasionally visited the earth. They certainly did today!" one station reported.

Another station showed crowds eager to show their gratitude, urging the priest at the heathen temples to declare this day Jupiter and Mercury Day, J and M Day, or simply JAM Day.

Still other channels highlighted the lavish parties, celebrity, and pop group invites, banners hung over expressways, TV infomerials, and decorative parades, with fireworks being readied for the big celebration.

Reporters from CNN mobile teams and the Associated Press quickly found where Paul and Barnabas were staying.

Paul and Barnabas looked at each other in disbelief.

Then it started—the banging on the door. Shouting reporters and filmmakers jamming mics and camera lenses near the crack in the door, waiting for it to open.

"We are waiting to see the gods!" one newscaster gleefully announced while smiling into cameras.

Then the two whipped their eyes toward the ceiling as the sound of circling news helicopters hovered above and shook the run-down motel. Searchlights streamed through the apartment windows, nearly blinding them.

Finally, Paul and Barnabas realized what was going on.

"This can't be!" Paul shouted with consternation.

In outrage he ripped his shirt. Barnabas did the same. As Paul opened the door, Barnabas plowed through the reporters like a NFL linebacker. With the force of adrenaline, they reached the street, leaving a trail of reporters in heaps of twisted microphones, cables, cameras, and bruised reporters. The two ran into the crowd of bystanders, waving and shouting for them to quiet.

Paul sensed the gathering mass of faces was expecting melodious acceptance and gracious thank-yous. But like seaweed against the mighty ocean currents, Paul continued waving his arms slowly for the crowd to quiet.

Finally the roar died down, and Paul spoke through a bull-horn handed him.

"Fine citizens of Lystra, why are you celebrating us?"

He looked from right to left.

"We are not gods! We are are just men like you. We came to you in the name of the Most High God, the God of heaven and earth, the one who gives light to the sky, power to thunder, and fire to lightning. He gives the wind its wings and gently sprinkles life upon plants and animals. His breath awakens life every living thing."

Paul paused for effect.

"Friends, He is the one who shows mercy and forgiveness to you who are blind and whose hearts long for hope."

There was a moment of quiet, like the eye of a cyclone, as the crowds murmured and shuffled.

Then Paul continued.

"It is He alone who is worthy of worship!"

Then the crowd exploded again into songs and chants.

Paul and Barnabas looked at each other and realized Paul's entreaty had fallen on deaf ears.

"We have seen the miracles!" a lady shouted from the crowd.

Another called, "We will make offerings and sacrifices to you, O Jupiter and Mercury!"

Paul and Barnabas realized nothing they could say would change the minds of the people. They returned to their apartment, through the tunnel of jostling reporters and bolted the door. They knelt, and prayed for wisdom for what to do next.

The electricity of the night before was still in the air of Lystra. The next morning, they were invited to a morning talk show. Leaving through the window and down the back fire-escape they made their way to the TV studio.

The cameras focused in on Paul as he spoke eloquently of the God of heaven. He told them how God had chosen them, simple earthly men, like any of those of Lystra. The message was to bring the good news of the true God's love, grace, and sacrifice through His son, Jesus Christ of Nazareth. Paul invited all watching the broadcast to believe and accept God's gift of eternal life.

The studio was deathly quiet. The program manager signaled the control room to cut the feed and stop the cameras.

"We will pause for comerical break," the newscaster apologized.

Paul knew his prayers had been answered as he saw the bewildered expressions and shocked facies of all who stood behind the cameras.

Paul knew the citizens of Lystra and Derbe finally realized he was telling the truth: they were not gods of Omlypus but merely men of Israel whose God was the God of the Jews.

In surrounding cities and across the nation, the morning talk shows aired the shocking news throughout the day. Many of the programs were hateful tirades of outrage that the impersonators had belittled the gods of Lystra.

Far away, shortly before sunset, certain Jews from Antioch and Iconium, along with JHS operatives, boarded a plane and flew to Lystra. The kill contract from the JHS was still secretly in effect for Agent Saul. There had been no changes.

At a meeting in the city council chambers the next afternoon, Jews from out of town persuaded the Jupiter and Mercury members that they could ill afford another public embarassement. They apologized, embellished their acquaintance with Paul and Baranbas, and affirmed them as herectics, rabble-rousers, blasphemers, enemies to the faith of Israel, and disrespectors of idol-god worshippers of Lystra.

Paul learned of this sometime later from an informant who owed Agent Saul a favor. Paul and Barnabas realized they had to move to a new location. They found an another low-cost motel near the outskirts of Lystra. The neighborhood was poor and oblivious to most things happening around it.

Paul was soundly sleeping on a sagging cot next to the motel window.

Barnabas, holding Paul's sunglasses, looked at his sleeping friend and smiled. For an ever so brief a moment he thought of tickling Paul's ear with a feather, but he paused to remember rumors of the quickness and lethality of the former Agent Saul. *I'd better leave him alone and let the flies die annoying him.*

A rare breeze of cool air gently lifted the curtains. The coolness deepened the sleep, turning off the sixth sense Paul usually had about his surroundings.

Barnabas left the apartment in the bright sunlight wearing the aviators and trying to look cool, but not obviously too cool. His stomach grumbled for a vegan sandwich and a can of cold orange juice. He was also anxious to get a newspaper up the street at the corner store.

As Barnabas walked, he thought, *The streets are unusually quiet. Where are all the people and cars?*

He paused, stepped into a locked doorway, and looked around.

He listened and thought, *What are those dogs barking at?*

Then he saw them: a squad of seven or eight men dressed in black with face shields and carrying MP5 submachine guns. They were silently moving toward the apartment he had just left.

He saw the leader using hand signals and gestures, directing the advancing masked SWAT team and JHS agents behind him. Above them on a rooftop across the street two teams of snipers and spotters.

The quiet of the street suddenly shook from the rattling blast of a flash-bang grenade inside the building where Paul was sleeping.

Within seconds, the startled and dazed Paul was bound with painful plastic wrist restraints, tape placed over his mouth and a burlap bag over his head.

Paul flinched as an agent kicked him in the stomach and spat tobacco juice on him. Paul did not struggle; he knew the drill. Struggling made things worse, if they could get worse.

Barnabas saw the flashing lights and the black SWAT carrier pull up in front of the motel. He knew what had happened. With chest heaving and fear rising like volcanic lava, he turned and disappeared down an alley.

Standing at the door of the SWAT carrier, the leader spoke into his radio. "Director Allen, we've got the target. What do you want us to do with him?"

He waited for a reply.

Director Allen, a short, aged, and balding man resembling the actor Danny DeVito, answered in his usual paranoid whisper. "Turn him over to those pagan dogs. Let them do the work. Keep our hands clean."

"Got it, sir," the SWAT leader replied dutifully.

The special extraction team drove the bound and blindfolded Paul some miles away from the city.

Paul felt the vehicle stop. The steel door of the carrier opened, and immediately he heard voices and shouts from angry people.

"Here he is, your Hanukkah present, all gift-wrapped," a soldier said, laughing.

The waiting Lystranian mob, including some Jews, welcomed their holiday present.

Paul was thrown to the ground. His memory rebounded to a few nights before when he'd listened to the demonic fury and fervor preparing to celebrate him and Barnabas.

His recollection was short-lived as he heard the SWAT carrier drive away. The mob started beating and kicking him.

"This is the guy who pretended to be a god!" he heard someone say.

Another called out, "Where's that other guy?"

"This one will do for now!" Laughter and cursing broke out.

Blindfolded and hurting badly, Paul could hardly determine whether this was a really bad dream or just a simple nightmare.

Paul tried to catch his breath between the yanking, pulling, and beating as they dragged him feet first, leaving his head and bound hands to scrape against sharp stones, and broken glass.

Night had settled on the deserted rural wasteland.

Flashlight beams sporadically swept across the blindfold, and from an open edge and the smell of gasoline, Paul knew he was near a gas station or truck stop.

The mob dragged him to an abandoned, burned-out gas station hidden from view by tall, dry grass, weeds, and rusted dumpsters.

Paul was dehydrated and felt like he was going to pass out.

For a moment, ever so brief, a hazy clarity surfaced in Paul's subconscious. It was a replay of a mind movie he'd seen a hundred times.

The film featured the martyr Stephen and him standing next to his black SUV. Now this ironic justice and role reversal had come full circle. Fate had come to pay its due.

Though the darkness and pain had nothing humorous in it, Paul's mind drifted away from Stephen, perhaps more of a way to protect itself from the inevitable. He began to hope that in all this day's scuffling, he had not lost or broken his sunglasses.

Pauls arms were jerked upward, and pain ravaged his spine as the mob stopped.

"This looks like a good spot," a voice announced.

Pauls eyes were covered with a dirty cheese cloth burlap; he could smell good old goat cheese anywhere, even here. The other thing not so welcome was the smell and taste of his own blood—a sharp bitterness that soured his mouth.

Then he heard the chains, the gathering of stones, and the whispers of, "Let's do this!"

He anticipated the coming storm, and it came, blow after blow.

In the receding echos of his attackers, just before unconscicousness, Paul wished for death.

He didn't remember when he stopped feeling the pain, or hearing the shouts of victory and celebration of his executioners. In his mind, he imagined not only those outside his mind but those inside, the ones from the memory movies. The dark watchers who stood beyond human sight and origin, the nebulous visitors of spiritual darkness and wickedness in high places. The unseen watchers of his imagination that look on him with cruelty and gratification.

Paul heard himself groan. Then he saw nothing, heard nothing, and felt nothing.

For Paul, time stopped.

There were no more mind movies, only silence and blackness. No more past and no more tomorrows.

A mob member bantered, "One last hit for good luck!" He kicked Paul in the head with his steel-toed boot.

Silence fell over the small patch of ground where the body lay. Crickets began to chirp. Night birds returned to signal the day's end.

The mob disappeared, lumbering like well-fed beasts into the night.

About ten minutes after the group vanished, the crickets suddenly stopped chirping, and black birds flittered from nearby trees. Across the dirt road from the gas station, a thicket of bushes rattled and then parted as dark shadows slowly moved toward the motionless body of Paul.

Barnabas led a small band of believers to claim the body of their beloved Paul.

"We must hurry before the wild dogs and coyotes come," someone whispered.

Finally the shadows encircled the body.

Barnabas kneeled near Paul and placed his hand on Paul's head.

"Sorry, brother. I wasn't there for you." He sniffled and rubbed his eyes.

Barnabas listened as others wept as quietly as they could. Barnabas also wept inside as he remembered his friend.

He was my brother and our hope. He was our connection with heaven, Barnabas reflected.

Staring at the dark hulk on the ground, Barnabas remembered Paul's quirky laugh and the snorting aftermath of funny jokes they shared. He smiled.

Then he smiled even more when he thought of the times they prayed together and the miracles that were wrought.

Barnabas stood up, holding the aviator sunglasses he'd borrowed. This was his last sacred possession from his lost companion. He didn't know what more to say or even think. He bowed his head and prayed simply.

"Father, Eternal, All-wise. The God who never makes a mistake.

The one who loves and cherishes His children, please help us this night to bear this grief. Amen."

Deep within Paul, a stirring arose. Dormant nerves once holding the treasure of memories began to blink again, brighter and brighter. Energizing microcurrents of life surged forward through dark corridors of nerves, muscles, and finally into the heart. With each spark of life, each pulse, the blood in Paul's vessels began to move, slowly at first and then faster.

Still locked just inside the door of consciousness, Paul heard noise like music, like singing, like voices beautiful, perfect and clear.

He sensed that it must be the melodic crescendo of angelic voices he imagined so many times when he and Banabas prayed. Then he heard another voice, a softer and familiar voice.

It was the voice from the Damascus road. The one who opened his blinded eyes and privileged him to behold the vistas of heaven. But more then anything else, it was the one who gave purpose to his life: to glorify God and share the Gospel with Gentiles.

"Paul, awake!" Jesus said. "You have shared in My suffering. Your faithfulness is recorded."

The Life-giver continued. "My son, I have much for you to do."

Then He commanded Paul, "Arise! I am with you always."

Paul sensed he might be able to move a little, but the awareness of the pain stopped him.

Those standing about him in the dark shuffled before bending to lift the body of Paul.

One of the shadows bent down to take hold of Paul's shoulders.

Then he fell back and shouted,"He's breathing!"

Quickly he covered his mouth as others reacted and backed away, startled.

In the dark, Paul's eyes remained closed.

One of the shadows, a young man of twenty or so, bent nervously down to feel Paul's neck for a pulse.

"I … I don't feel …"

Then he stopped mid-sentence as Paul suddenly grabbed his hand and with a raspy voice asked, "Who are you?"

Freightened, the youthful voice stuttered, "I … I'm T-Timothy, son of Eunice, th-the grandson of Lois."

CHAPTER EIGHT

TIMOTHY

Then Moses said to the Lord, "O my Lord, I am not eloquent, neither before nor since You have spoken to Your servant; But I am slow of speech and slow of tongue."

So the Lord said to him, "Who has made man's mouth … Have not I, the Lord? Now therefore, go, and I will be with your mouth and teach you what you shall say." (Exodus 4:10–12 NIV)

Eunice smiled as she looked down on her squirming bundle of joy with flashing gray eyes. The infant with smooth caramel skin looked back in quiet wonderment.

"Jacob, he has eyes like your grandfather," she said softly to her husband.

Timothy—or Tim, as everyone called him—sported gray eyes that were irresistibly alluring and mesmerizing. The eyes garnered admiration even as a baby. Tim's eyes did not go unnoticed by the other children, particularly by girls and ladies in years to come.

"What's his name again?" Jacob asked playfully.

Eunice whispered, never taking her hazel eyes off his sparkling grays, "Timothy."

"And from my family." Jacob tapped his chest proudly and declared, "He will be of the tribe of Judah."

With quiet affirmation, Eunice added, "And from my family, he will have his name." She smiled.

The name Timothy in Greek meant "God's honor." Beyond his undistinguished beginning, he was no less a champion and recipient of God's abiding, qualifying, and sustaining grace.

His grandmother Lois taught him daily the things of God through stories and illustrations from nature as she held him, then pushed him in a stroller, and then held his little hand as they walked through the parks.

Eunice and Lois protected Tim as much as they could from those who made fun of his one great nemesis that would plague him throughout his life: his stuttering.

Despite what others viewed as a handicap, God nevertheless placed within Tim's heart the counsel, "Be not thou therefore ashamed of the testimony of our Lord … For God has not given us the spirit of fear; but of power, and love, and of a sound mind" (2 Timothy 1:7–8). With these words, Lois would comfort Tim.

So began the amazing story of storms and grace in the life of Timothy from the tribe of Judah.

Long before that faithful night when young Timothy stood among the shadowy figures retrieving the battered body of Paul, his own life began thousands of miles away in the narrow streets of an American city called Detroit.

Detroit was famous for its automobile factories and was the birthplace of R&B music; folks there and around the world simply called it Motown.

The city's teeming core near downtown Detroit was mostly poor people of varying shades of light to dark skin. It was derisively called the Black Bottom and was the territory of the notorious Purple

Gang, which vied for control of the liquor and gambling business with Chicago gangster Al Capone.

In areas away from the inner city were skin shades, much lighter and some darker, made an ethnic cocktail of immigrants from Poland, the Middle East, India, and Pakistan lived the other half of Detroit's melting pot. They lived in communities that were fiercely territorial and enjoyed a life rich from the exploitation of the city's poor far away from their idyllic enclaves.

Amid all the social storms of the time, an oasis was found in the neighborhood where Tim grew up.

The quilted fabric of that neighborhood was made up of the poor and less poor, factory workers, maids, crafty mothers, wizened old people, an assortment of harmless drunks, hip-hop damaged teens, and hundreds of half-clothed, noisy, very dusty kids; this was Waterloo Street.

Tim's two-block world was bound to the east by McDougal Street, to the north by Vernor Highway, to the west by Joseph Campau Street, and to the south by Jay Street.

This was his playground, an incubator of character, a wonderful world of adventure and imagination. It was a safe place to be a kid.

On Waterloo Street, the children could be anything they wanted to be. They could flash wooden swords like Zorro, swing from garage to garage on stolen cloth line like Tarzan, sing like the O'jays on street corners at night, pretend to be Denzel and steal a kiss, explore the galaxies for treasures lying in back alleys like Luke Skywalker, or wrestle for the championship in dirt and mud like Dwayne "The Rock" Johnson. A thousand characters, a thousand visions of hero-ism each day through play while being children who were protected and loved.

Waterloo was for so many kids the birthplace of bright tomor-rows, a safe place to be a kid, to grow up, to survive in the world that lay beyond the borders of their neighborhood world.

For some it was all that, yet for others the future disappeared into a dark cloud of time and reality.

As time passed, the children grew up and ventured beyond their past. Some went off to distant wars and never returned. Drugs, alcohol, and the bitter taste of racial tension coiled about the lives of many like a python strangling the joy and happiness they once knew. It became the reality that spared few.

The shelter that was once Waterloo became the graveyard of blighted dreams, the silent echoes of children playing, and tragically the hoofs of wild stallions rushing madly to a hellish end called change.

But while time and love sheltered Tim, Waterloo was the place of learning, of growing, the kiln of testing fires. It was the place where scaffolding hardness was forged, the place where endurance and tenacity welded the steel girders of Tim's life to stand the winds of time and change—and even more, to weather the storms that so surely came.

As Tim grew, the neighborhood also grew. It became older and changed. And in the world of others, beyond Waterloo, there was little warmth or compassion.

"Handicap, disabled, freak, jacked-up," and other insults were disguised in concealed laughter. Some more open and painful and mocking; "Oh my god, what a shame. He needs to shut up. Dude give it a rrrrrest!" The cruelty from such for all stutterers was ever present.

Those who mocked were themselves not without their own handicaps, some not so visible or crippling yet just as socially weakening. Theirs was a personal and painful emotional sore that secretly gnawed at their own human frailty, their scabs of imperfection. Ignorantly, their defense was the need to transfer attention away, toward someone else more visible, more defenseless than themselves—the convenient release to ease what they could not change.

Tim did not always stutter. Except for the Eternal everything has a beginning.

Tim's grandmother, Lois, tried to explain to Tim why he stuttered to comfort him. But it was more to assure him that God would one day fix everything.

Tim remembered much of what his grandmother told him and also remembered how he felt.

When Tim's uncle Oden, Jacob's older brother, a fuel delivery man, backed his growling coal truck into the driveway, the terror would begin. If in January, when the truck growled, the January morning suddenly grew colder. Three-year-old Tim's eyes would flash open at the familiar sound. If already up and dressed, his tiny bare feet would freeze to the floor right where he stood. His twiggy brown legs vibrated like guitar strings, and a stream of pee pooled at his feet.

Listening, Tim would hear Uncle Oden push past the creaking iron gate. His tiny heart pounded desperately, tearing against his heaving chest and trying to escape, but his paralyzed body would not move. Tim wished he could leave his body behind and hide somewhere, anywhere away from Uncle Oden. His gray eyes wild with panic, Tim would again plead with his legs to run, but the cement of fear held them tighter than ever. His lungs heaved and swelled, trying to get enough air to call for help, but his throat blocked the summons of rescue. Tim knew his uncle would come straight to him as he always did.

Uncle Oden delivered wood, coal, and heating oil to houses mostly in the black neighborhoods of Detroit. His coveralls reeked of pungent fuel oil and a powdery coating of black coal dust and soot.

Uncle Oden, a well-nourished, rotund man who loved Cadillac cars, vacations to places poor people could not afford, and the admiring accolades at the pagan temple he enjoyed each Sunday. These made him happy. His daily ritual of terror on Tim also made him happy. His work was hard, and this bogeyman play made him laugh; it was his stress reliever. He thought it insanely funny.

The creaking metal gate ... then in through the back door, and with slow, exaggerated pounding footsteps, he'd ascend the four wooden steps into the kitchen. After bursting into the kitchen with arms raised and growling like a grizzly bear, he'd shout, "Where's my boy?"

Even Eunice, Tim's mom, would jump at times from his antics. "Stop doing that!" she'd scream.

This only fed into his happy moment. He'd laughed louder and then bellow, "Where's my boy!"

Horrified, Tim's eyes slammed shut to hide the monster, but the approaching monster's earthquake footsteps forced his eyes open again. Then he'd shut them once more, praying the beast would go away.

Grabbing Tim under his arms, Uncle Oden would lift him up past his pearly teeth, high above his head. Then he'd lower him to eye level, the miniature frame shivering uncontrollably. The quivering would transition to rigidity, and Tim would become stiff as a stick.

Uncle Oden stood like a towering tree where lived two large owlish eyes buried in the blackness of a bough, glaring, staring, and taunting Tim. To bring the theatrics to a close, Uncle Oden would rub his coal-dusted griminess all over the tiny face. Throwing his head back, Uncle Oden would let out a thunderous laugh at Tim's fresh morning makeup of coal dust.

This was Tim's childhood nightmares, week after week. This was the beginning, and at the mention of Uncle Oden's name, Tim shook violently, cried, and began staccato pleas for help. So it was that the stuttering began and never left him.

For many, that was simply bad karma or dumb luck, but for Tim it became his focus and determination to overcome.

Stuttering made him deeply frustrated and reluctant to speak in school and at home, and it even caused him to avoid playing with other children for fear of ridicule.

His mother Eunice and Grandmother Lois were his sources of comfort. They reminded him that by trusting Yahweh, all things were possible, even learning to speak without stuttering. They squeezed the bitter lemon of stuttering into the sweet lemonade of faith.

At sunset each Friday, the start of the Jewish Sabbath, the family would gather together to sing; it was the best time. Surprisingly, Tim never stuttered when singing. Perhaps he felt more relaxed because he loved the gift of music from God.

In school Tim began to excel in his studies, especially math, science, and physics. He was a loner to some extent, and this allowed him to concentrate and compensate where other students floundered from distractions of popularity and social media.

He didn't own a cell phone or have a Twitter or Facebook account. His stuttering, however, was captured on Snapshot listings, mimicking videos, and stolen background selfies by others. He was called a mime, the Mute, and Weirdo. To some of his classmates who rudely avoided him, he was a "machine gun" of verbal embarrassment.

Miraculously, all of this began to disappear when a few unfortunates discovered something really special about Tim: he could fight like a maniac. To Lois and Eunice, this was not a gift.

Another amazing thing people learned about him was he could swim and dive like an Olympian.

In high school, his muscular build, broad shoulders, infectious smile, and blossoming personality made him quite handsome. With more confidence, Tim tried and mastered nearly every sport. His athletic bent earned praise, popularity, and acceptance. But none of this held any importance to Tim. His mind was set only to please God. As he honored God, so was he honored by the Almighty.

Timothy became the high school's diving champion, winning more trophies and awards than any other student in school history.

Tim hated the attention he received from the physical things he did. He wanted people to know him as a person. He never forgot the wisdom of his grandmother Eunice reminding him, "Always put God first, and you'll never be last."

Time and living never slows down. The past quickly becomes the future in a moment. The casualty of time is that as moments disappear, so do important people, places, and even relationships.

The Detroit auto industry crashed from corporate greed, robotics and overseas out-sourcing of manufacturing.

Many workers were unable to support their families and so transferred to other locations. Some sought overseas oil and construction jobs in Saudi Arabia and other parts of the Middle East, where the pay was higher but the jobs more riskier.

Jacob's family moved from Detroit to Lystra in southern Turkey. It was there that Eunice and Lois came in contact with followers of the Way.

The family except for Jacob, who went on to work in the oil fields, had been following CNN news stories about the Nazarene who was crucified in Jerusalem. They were amazed at the rumors of dead people returning to life, and news of the rampaging persecution of heretics by the Jewish Security Forces. Like much on TV and the *Jewish Enquirer* tabloid, it sounded like gossip and hearsay.

As it happened, while at a flea market one day, a very kind lady selling sandals and pottery invited them to friendship meetings at her small home on the edge of town not far from where they lived.

At one of the meetings, a guest named Peter and several other men, recounted the story of the Nazarene they'd heard about on TV. Captivated and convicted at the same time, the trio of Lois, Eunice, and Timothy listened with rising excitement that they had found the long-awaited Messiah. From that time on, they continued meeting, sharing, and supporting other followers of the Way.

When not helping in the community, Eunice worked with the telephone company, and Lois took care of the house and cooking.

Timothy now attended the University of Lystra (UOL) with a full swimming scholarship. His major was mechanical engineering, and from day one students and faculty knew Timothy, the son of Jacob, the Greek from the tribe of Judah was special.

His popularity grew even more despite his efforts to stay low key. One of his favorite hobbies was computer programming; it proved a way of making a little extra cash. He created a dating software program for students on campus. Some of the matches were questionable, but like the disclaimer before signing up read, "Programmer not responsible for results or children who resemble someone else." It was all in fun and was a much-welcomed release from the stress of university studies.

Swimming was always a challenge and a joy for Tim. With the new success of the swim team since Tim's arrival, the coach demanded more of his athletes, Tim included.

The University of Lystra was a state-owned university with many wealthy sponsors and contributors to the school's programs and trust fund.

At the beautiful entrance of the university stood a huge silver and bronze statue of the god Jupiter on a platform holding lightning bolts pointing to the high arched entrance gate. The grassy campus lawn seemed to go on forever. Pygmy shade trees dotted the campus along the cobblestone walkways, some covered with leafy vines in places.

Adding to the affluent decor were marble fountains here and there to throw coins into for luck. The ornate walls and buildings pictured carved images of the various gods and scenes of the Peloponnesian war between Athens and Sparta.

At night the fountains glowed from lights set deep and at different angles in the water, giving soft hues of reds, blues, yellows, and greens that faded in and out, creating a festive mood to the evenings.

To top off the elegance of the opulent campus, peacocks with their fanned emerald tails roamed freely while pink flamingos balanced gracefully on one leg in ponds that bordered the campus.

The idyllic beauty of the walk to the swim building at the athletic complex gave no warning to Tim as he strolled into the building one particular day.

"Hey, Tim," Coach Johnson called. "Can I have a word with you in my office?"

The coach stared Tim squarely in the eyes to see his reaction to his next words.

"I know because of your mother's Jewish faith, you keep their Sabbath on Friday nights and have declined swimming competitions on Saturdays. And I know our recruiter promised you'd never have to swim at those times … But the team needs you to swim."

Seeing Tim's face slack a little, he turned his gaze down at his own rotating thumbs.

"National competitions are coming, and we need you to swim and dive on …"

"Coach," Tim interrupted. "I-I appreciate everything you've d-done, b-but I can't disobey God or my con-con-conscience."

Coach slammed his fist on the desk. "You'll lose your scholarship, son! What's more important?"

Tim sat quietly and uneasy.

Returning the coach's glance briefly, he stood and walked out the office. On the way back to the dorm, Tim didn't question his decision.

The sun shone brightly in the cloudless sky, birds sang, and a slight breeze rustled the vines as Tim passed under them. In his mind's eye, he saw Grandma Lois holding his tiny cheeks in her hands and saying, "Timmy, make God first in your life, and you'll never be last at anything." Those words gave him courage then and even more so now. He knew he had made the right decision. But looming deep in his conscience, another voice mocked and assured him that from his teammates and fans, he would find no comfort and no solace.

Posters all over campus announced the coming championship swim meet.

A number of weekends had passed since the threat from Coach Johnson and Tim's ban from the pool. The swim team worked hard to adjust to the absence of Timothy. He was not only their best diver and inspiration, but he was their undeclared team leader. They admired him for his skills and respected his faith. Before events, Tim would bow his head to pray silently to himself, and he always included his teammates. Some of his teammates were clearly not religious but would often fake a look at their feet with bowed heads, pretending to stretch their toes.

Tim received consolation from his mom and grandmother, but he was even more thankful for the letters he received from his friend Paul.

Ever since that night at the burned-out gas station, a new friendship had forged between Timothy and the apostle Paul. Paul kept track of Timothy's progress through school and the nonsense stuff on Facebook. He sent occasional letters boasting how proud he was of Timothy, and each time he ended his letter asking Timothy to join him after graduation on his missionary journeys. That was always a cherished moment. Tim took courage after reading Paul's letters.

The day for the first round of competition came. It was a disaster. The team from Antioch University gave Lystra U their A-game. The embarrassing second and third place standings for Lystra were celebrated by the fans with boos and heckles.

Intermission between swim sets brought a few minutes of quiet and reflection. Coach Johnson stood solemnly in the corner near the shower door, looking at the idle diving board. The coach could take this humiliation no longer. He went to his office and make some phone calls.

Across campus, Tim sat on a bench beneath one of the pygmy shade trees. He didn't see Coach Johnson walking toward him through the thick grass.

"Tim," the coach said, startling Tim, who fumbled and dropped his calculus book.

"We'd like you to come back." Coach paused a moment and then hesitantly extended his hand.

"I talked with the National Swim Committee, and they agreed to reschedule all our events for week-days and Sundays. No messing with the Sabbath. What do you think?"

A broad smile blossomed across young Timothy's face.

"Thank you, Coach!" He returned the handshake. Then Tim shouted, "Thank You, God!"

He turned and dashed across the campus to the swim team locker room. Hardly stopping to take a quick shower, he grabbed his swim trunks and, without looking, put them on backwards. He burst through the doors into the pool area and dove into the crystal blue water, swimming, diving, and singing praises to God.

CHAPTER NINE

RECRUITMENT

When the dented Ford pickup with oxidized paint, a shattered front headlight, and a hanging muffler clattered to a smoking stop in front of Timothy's, apartment everybody turned to stare.

Timothy was awakened from sleep by the noise, and he squinted in the blinding morning light at the rising exhaust that looked like a vehicle on fire.

From the smoke appeared a dark-haired man wearing sunglasses and a dusty black leather jacket.

"Brother Paul!" Timothy shouted excitedly, smashing his head against the open window.

Paul looked up and smiled.

From the other side of the choking cloud, two other figures like ghostly apparitions appeared: Silas and Dr. Luke. Both were coughing and covering their noses with Bedouin scarves.

Slightly shorter then Paul and a little heavier, Silas wore a safari jacket. He stepped into view first. Silas, his nickname, was short for Silvanus Bella, which meant "of the forest." His family lived in the dense cedar forests of Lebanon and were deer and boar hunters. He was Paul's new sidekick.

Barnabas had left on another missionary assignment to Cyprus with a young believer named John Mark.

Paul and Barnabas talked often by cell phone and texted each other, reporting how the churches were doing and recalling old times and humor that still made them laugh.

Silas, Paul's companion in ministry, was a seasoned worker and was gifted with the spirit of prophecy. The work to be done was so great that there was need of training more laborers for active service and Silas was the man for the job.

In Timothy, Paul saw one who appreciated the sacredness of the work of a minister. Tim was not appalled at the prospect of suffering and persecution, and he was willing to be taught. Yet the apostle did not venture to take the responsibility of giving Timothy, an untried youth, training in the Gospel ministry without first fully satisfying himself in regard to his character and his past life.[2]

Luke Gardner was a medical doctor. He was thin but muscular. His rough, tanned face was weathered by years of sun and desert, and he sported a well-trimmed mustache and kind brown eyes.

In his youth before medical school, Luke had been a decorated combat medic in the Israeli Defense Force (IDF). It was later that he met Agent Saul, now Paul, while they worked at Jewish Homeland Security. Dr. Luke became a believer after working cases at the JHS and interviewing numerous people who had known the one they called Jesus. He kept detailed records, recordings, and photos. Some of his pictures appeared in *National Geographic*. It was the research that eventually convinced him he could no longer work as an agent with the JHS. Unlike the supernatural conversion of Saul, Dr. Luke was convicted by the Spirit of God and the remarkable testimonies of many believers. The most inspiring discovery was the faith and willingness of many to die for their belief, declaring that God had a better place for them.

The trip to the city of Lystra was not just a social call to check on the believers there. They came to get Timothy. After the hugs, hand slapping, and fist bump rituals that guys do, they told Timothy why they'd come and why they needed him.

---

[2] Acts of the Apostles, p. 203.

As they talked, Timothy could hear the theme from the movie *Mission Impossible* drumming in his head. His knee started shaking, and his fingers thumped on the table in sync with the mental tune.

"Tim," Paul interrupted the private concert. "What do you think? Are you with us, son? I talked with your mom and grandma, Lois, a couple days ago. They were a little concerned but realized God was calling you to a higher service."

The music stopped. "Y-yes. Wouldn't miss it for the world!" Timothy blurted, and then he grinned his classic grin.

Two weeks later, they were headed for Syria, Cilicia, and Troas.

While in Troas, Paul was awakened in the middle of the night by a figure dressed in the style of a poor factory worker. The man was holding a Bible and pleading for Paul to come to East Macedonia to help the believers.

The next day, after ditching the pickup that nobody would buy, they boarded a Mediterranean fishing trawler headed for Philippi in the province of Macedonia, Greece.

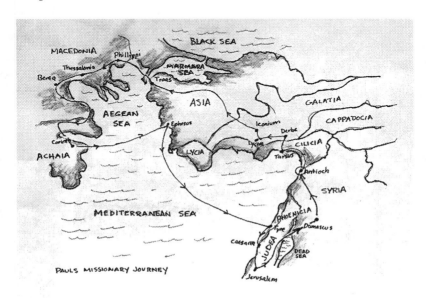

PAUL'S MISSIONARY JOURNEY

CHAPTER TEN

MISS JAMA

"Call me noow fo ya free readin'," the yellow-turbaned black lady spoke, her eyes flashing at the TV camera in front of her. The psychic hotline was a nightly ritual for the superstitious people of Philippi.

To the network executives, she was worth millions. Miss Jama, for sixty dollars per call, would shuffle her tarot cards, scatter chicken bones, or massage her crystal ball and then droll out advice on love, relationships, and fortune. To some of the faithful, she guaranteed curses for enemies or spurned lovers. To the grieving, she gave believable messages from the dead and to the insomniacs positive meanings to nightmares if they paid with a credit card. For those who paid by check she gave ambiguous meanings until the check cleared the bank.

Miss Jama said, and she corrected no one even when reporters found otherwise, that she was from the island of Jamaica, but actually she was born in Needles, California, to parents from Trinidad. The family left the Caribbean because of little Bouree Bell Jamona (Miss Jama's real name).

There were reflective moments when Miss Jama would stare into the crystal ball and reminisce on her own dark childhood. She thought of times like back in Trinidad and Tobago.

Whenever they visited family and few friends in Trinidad,

there was always trouble. Not unlike when families gather for Thanksgiving dinner and all the dark and shameful feeling spew across turkey with dressing, cranberry sauce and wine glasses. Folks always came around to saying, "That Bouree was a demon child."

Trancelike and with the habit of a forty-year-old, her tongue always found that spot just inside of her upper lip where the scar was—the scar she was innocent of, the one she didn't deserve.

She was about three years old. She remembered walking with her mother and meeting Father Cane, the local parish priest.

"Bouree, say hello to the father," Bouree's mother said to her cautiously, never knowing what would come out of her mouth from one moment to the next.

Miss Jama stared and remembered. *That's what pain does: it cause you to remember. A thousand good things can happen, but pain always makes you remember.*

Little Bouree looked the priest squarely in the eye and then lowered her eyes. "Da spirits say you do bad things in the night wit yo' thing, there," she said, pointing to his private area.

Bouree's mother pursed her lips and then immediately slapped her across the mouth, the head, and the back. "Child! Tell the father you're sorry!" she screamed.

Blood poured from the Bouree's lip and nose as she cried, "It true, what dey tell me, Mama." She cried harder. "It true!"

Embarrassed, the priest reached nervously to loosen his white collar and stared down at Bouree. Feigning surprise, he suggested the child needed exorcism and discipline.

Bouree sensed others were afraid of her and her "gift." Children were not allowed to play with her, and teachers always separated her from the other students. The whole community shunned the family with the demon child.

Eventually the family left the islands for good, moved back to California, and then moved as far away as they could from those who knew their past. The coastal city of Philippi, on the Aegean Sea in southern Greece, was the perfect place where such rumors could be profitable and nobody cared about the past.

Bouree, or Miss Jama as she called herself now, spoke perfect English, but the island accent seemed to give her a sense of being special and mysterious. Besides, people liked the novelty of the accent. They trusted her, willingly paid more, and believed she indeed had supernatural powers of perception and contact with the departed.

Like her fellow soothsayers, John Edwards from the American TV show *Crossing Over* and columnist Jean Dickson, along with fifty other less prominent merchants of darkness, they all knew the big time was to be on *Larry King Live*. And if Larry King was the holy grail of TV, then being in Philippi—the heart of witchcraft, the capital of Middle East Voodoo, and the center of trendy superstitions—was the place to be if one wanted to get rich.

Paul, Silas, Dr. Luke, and Timothy were well received in the city of Philippi. The believers praised God for sending this evangelistic team at such a critical time when apostasy, waning morale, and discord were taking its toll.

Immediately Dr. Luke and Timothy organized health seminars, cooking classes, community service clubs, and visitation programs.

Paul and Silas preferred the streets. They went into the heart of the city, the fashion row district, the Wall Street areas, the manicured neighborhoods of the rich, the wood and tin-roofed dwelling of the destitute, and the festive enclave of magic shops, fortune readers, séance parlors, and street magicians. This was where they met Miss Jama.

Once or twice a week, Miss Jama performed a live street broadcast. The TV production truck and studio van with dangling antennae and satellite dishes, sat among long black cables stretched across narrow streets like giant snakes.

Being seen and heard among the street people was her favorite time. The flare for the exotic and mysterious was her forte. She loved the attention and loved the money—lots of money.

In the middle of some advice to a caller, Miss Jama peered around the microphone dangling in front of her. She noticed through the Plexiglas window of the broadcast van a crowd of people around two men a short distance away. That was not disturbing, except that some of her followers were leaving her and walking toward the enlarging crowd near the strangers.

"See ya next time, darling," the psychic said before she turned off the mic. Waving to her production manager, she asked, "Who dem dat take away me business?"

The manager said, "Those guys are preachers from out of town."

"What day do here?" A furrow slowly ceased her forehead.

"I don't know, Miss Jama," the manager said, adjusting his headphones. "I heard them talk about a man who died and was raised from the dead."

Miss Jama placed her hand on her chin, leaned back in her chair, and mused at how she could make money out of this distraction.

Her specialty was dead people, so her mind began to calculate how a mutual business arrangement could work out for them.

Telling her production crew she was taking a break, Miss Jama left the booth and headed straight for the crowd gathering to hear the evangelists Paul and Silas.

Trailing Miss Jama was her own entourage of fifty or sixty psychic believers.

"Hey, you!" Miss Jama shouted as she pointed her diamond-studded index finger. "I know you!"

The words, the deep, eerie voice that came out of her mouth, startled even her as she stopped within a few feet of Paul and Silas. Immediately she sensed she was not in control of her mind or body. She was a bystander being controlled remotely from somewhere else inside of her.

"I know Jesus too!" the voice continued.

Miss Jama sensed her mouth moving, but it was not the words she thought.

"We can work together for the good people of Philippi," the voice continued.

Miss Jama felt as though she was watching a movie of herself, but another being was playing her part.

Paul looked at Silas and was about to speak when, from within the mass of the curious crowd, there started chanting, clapping of hands, and praising.

"The spirit world and the God of the Jews are united!"

"Give us wisdom and good fortune!"

Paul felt a coldness as he remembered the same demonic spirit entering the people of Lystra. They had nearly taken his life.

"Brother Paul," Silas said urgently, taking Paul by the arm. "Let's go!"

They forced their way through the frenzied crowd, hailed a cab, and disappeared down a ramp and onto the freeway.

The following week, the two evangelists gathered near the city hall. There was a small round marble platform where citizens could speak freely or musicians could play for donations. As before, a curious crowd gathered. Paul preached Jesus Christ crucified, risen, and glorified. He gave the testimony of his former life as a JHS agent, the mercy of forgiveness God had granted him, and his appointment to deliver the good news to Jews and Gentiles. His appeal was that there was hope and freedom from sin and witchcraft for all who would accept Jesus not only as Savior but also as the Lord of their lives.

Then out of nowhere came a familiar voice from the TV. "Hey, man!" the psychic shouted. "I done found you!" Miss Jama stood in the open sunroof of her stretch gold limo.

Inside, a smaller entourage also bellowed from the rolled-down tinted windows of her limousine. "Praise be to God!" Within moments, the limo doors opened, and the admirers poured out.

Getting out last, she was dressed ceremoniously in a long silver dress and draped with a white Russian mink around her shoulders. She waded through the crowd and was about to speak when from within her the voice took charge again.

"I know you, servants of the Most High God!" With deepening menace the voice continued "Work with us or leave us alone!"

Without responding, Paul raised both his arms and bowed his head. "Father," he spoke softly, "free Your child from the demons that imprison her. Only You can do this" He paused a moment. "Make Your mighty power known to her and those who stand here today. Lord Jesus, hear me that You may be glorified."

Then Paul looked at Miss Jama and placed his hand on her head. "In the name of Jesus, demons, come out of her!"

The crowd stood paralyzed. The very air dared not stir. The usual noisy pigeons and squirrels vying for food in the park sat motionless and obedient. Time seemed to stand still as the crowd watched in amazement.

Miss Jama stood mute and frozen as a deer caught in the headlights of a semi. Having no more strength to stand, she slowly slumped to her knees. The white fur slid off her shoulders and onto the ground as if now worthless. Tears began to well up from her exhausted eyes. The circle of blue mascara mixed with glitter ran down her cheeks like falling stars. The voices were gone.

Paul gently reached to lift her, and their eyes met. He softly said, "Daughter, you are free."

CHAPTER ELEVEN
THE CROWD

The Santa Ana winds of California that fanned horrific wildfires could not have spread any faster than the news on social media, cellphone camera footage, and bystander accounts of that day. It was the day Miss Jama became a born-again Christian.

She was seen being baptized in the Aegean Sea, singing gospel music at a small church, and gathering and feeding homeless at the shelter.

The network executives were in a panic. Sponsors cancelled commercial contracts. Other prominent folks in the business of the occult quarreled among themselves about how best to contain the disaster. Company stocks fell hundreds of points, and small magic and paraphernalia shops were losing customers to the strangers who preached Jesus. Something had to be done—and done by any means necessary.

Paul and Silas heard the mob before they saw them. It was just after glorious sunset after a long day of witnessing. The two were tired but hyped from having a wonderful day of inviting the Philippians to know Jesus. They were not far from their apartment and so decided to walk and enjoy the night air.

On either side of the street were six-story brownstone tenements and a few mom-and-pop stores, along with the neighborhood beauty and barbershop. Parking was a premium, and so cars lined up bumper to bumper along its corridor with little room for passing traffic.

Stopping instinctively, they looked at each other, looked back, and then looked forward. Though he was now Paul, Agent Saul's street smarts and skills were still alive and well. Paul noticed that a truck at the front street had rolled up and blocked traffic. He looked back, and a dark SUV blocked the other end of the street. Car horns started honking and headlights flashed. Threading their way through the trapped cars was the frenzied mob.

In Paul's mind, they were like an apocalyptic zombie horde that had contracted a disease and were killing and mutating their victims into more zombies.

This crowd was not diseased but demon processed. Paul's mind raced for an answer as to what to do. By himself he could outmaneuver the crowd, but Silas could not run, jump, or climb as he could. In the past, he would have drawn his Glock-17 or a submachine pistol and gotten some instant respect. But now he was no longer dependent on his abilities, his skills, or his training. He depended on God. He and Silas spoke a quick prayer.

Within moments, the tidal wave of angry people tore past trapped drivers in cars and over hoods and roofs of cars, trampling the fallen ones. They moved past the brownstones and the stores, banging, shouting, and screaming, "Kill them! Kill them!" The horde came from both directions, and within seconds the two disappeared under the tsunami of kicks and vicious blows to their faces and heads. Paul felt his clothes being ripped and felt pain all over his body. He couldn't see Silas, who was grunting and moaning, barely audible over the din of the mob in the darkness of trampling legs and feet.

Every now and then, the streetlight allowed him a glimpse of two JHS agents standing on the steps of a brownstone, watching. Before the avalanche of beating started, Paul had noticed a police squad car idling on a side street before they'd turned the corner. It all clicked now. Paul knew the drill because they were the same orders he had received and given a hundred times: do nothing.

Paul prayed for a quick death, and then he heard the gunshot. The kicking and pounding stopped instantly. Light from the utility pole came across his face as he looked up through swollen eyes and into the face of Sergeant Meleck, now Chief Agent Meleck. He was holding his Glock-27 firmly in both hands. Before passing out, Paul heard, "That's enough!"

Agent Meleck glared at the crowd and dared anyone else to rise a hand against these two. "Take one more step, and I'll put a bullet between your eyes!"

The crowd backed away from the bloody missionaries. The agent remembered his boss and friend. Something inside him could not let his friend die like that. Agent Meleck pointed his automatic and commanded five or six of the men to pick up Paul and Silas and put them in the cruiser that was parked near the corner. Meleck scooped up the ripped black leather jacket, checked the inside pocket, and found the sunglasses amazingly unbroken.

He and the other JHS agent knew they couldn't disobey orders completely without consequences, and so they took Paul and Silas, now regaining consciousness, to the local jail for first aid and safety until they could figure out what to do next.

"At least they will be ok there for a while," Meleck said unconvincingly to his partner. Sitting in the front passenger seat, he turned and glanced briefly at Paul, then out the front window. He sat quietly staring and wondering what had changed his former boss. What had happened on that Damascus road? In his mind he asked, *Is there something to this religious stuff that I need in my own life?*

CHAPTER TWELVE

WE ARE HERE

The Watch Master, or jailer, received Paul and Silas from Meleck with no questions about the details of why they were brought there. The jailer was big, like a Russian with a barrowed chest, and cold dark beady eyes. His face was joyless. He was the sort on whom no one wasted greeting gestures, handshakes or polite smiles. He'd never bother to return the courtesy.

Within minutes four of his equally large associates dragged the two missionaries to a holding area, where several other guards sat outside the cells smoking cigarettes, drinking coffee, and playing cards.

The rusted jail door was opened, and they were deposited against one wall and anchored there by wrist and leg irons.

The jail was filthy with rat droppings, graffiti walls, and peeling paint long overdue for repainting. Those inmates who had been there the longest seemed immune to the overwhelming ammonia smell of urine-soaked floors. Even the putrid air rift with pungent aromas of unemptied buckets of human waste and vomit caused no reaction. If there was any good thing in all of this, it was that those once shiny buckets, little amenities of convenience, were hidden in the shadows of dark corners. What Paul could not see or smell, he could hear: swarming flies feasting, humming and happy.

In other parts of the jail block were other unfortunates. From lightless cells, Paul could hear them clamoring, cursing, and raking the bars with their chains. Some pleaded for water while others wanted cigarettes.

Up front in the receiving area, Meleck stood inches away from the jailer. Each looked at each other without blinking.

"Don't let nothin' happen to him before I get back in the morning. Got it?" Meleck warned without expression.

The jailer's eyes said nothing. He simply nodded and then smirked. Meleck, starred back at him. Their looks were those of hardened mercenaries, trained killers who understood the Code, and neither was intimidated by the other.

The two JHS agents backed toward the door, never taking their hands far from their weapons. They got into their vehicle and drove away into the night.

The jailer locked the door and went back to the area where Paul and Silas were chained. Walking to the square window in the cell door, he sarcastically introduced himself. "Well, boys, it's playtime before bed." He laughed loudly.

Behind him, the other bored guards suddenly came alive. They liked playtime. It broke the boredom and was their vent for low wages and filthy surroundings (to which they nonchalantly contributed).

"Let's try the battery-to-feet thing," one said, laughing.

"Nah, enough with that feet stuff," another said. "How 'bout some creativity? Headphones first, then the battery thing?"

"Yeah, that's cool!" They all laughed roughly.

The metal cell door swung open, and Paul and Silas were blinded by a bright spotlight recessed in the ceiling. The blindfolds hung around their necks. Paul tried to stand but was pulled back down by the handcuffs attached to the wall and his wrists. "Friends, brothers, why are you doing this?" he asked.

"I ain't yo' friend, and I ain't yo' brother!" scolded one of the guards, who laid a heavy slap to the side of Paul's head.

Bulky black headphones were placed over Paul's and Silas's ears while thick red and black cables from a row of eight or nine 12-volt truck batteries were attached to their bare feet with clamps.

"Wake up, fool," one guard said as he kicked Silas. "Wake up and enjoy the music."

They all laughed like kids on a playground, bullying and taunting the new kid.

"Nothing calms the soul like screamin' babies!" a guard joked. Then he howled like a wolf.

"Yeah!" another chimed in. "How 'bout a little heavy metal too?"

The group of jailers exploded in laughter and hoorahs.

Paul stilled himself for what he knew was about to happen. But despite his best effort, it didn't help.

The electric jolts grabbed and twisted every muscle in his body like the bite of a thousand snakes. The bites gorged deeply and then released, only to bite again.

Paul seized, vomited, and urinated. Unable to control any part of himself, he tried to find that secret place inside himself, his safe house, which they taught agents at JHS Interrogation School. It was the place where the mind could escape, lock itself up, and turn off the pain.

But this time he was lost in a world of pain. He could not find the safe house. His lungs ached, and his vocal chords shrieked involuntarily.

Two minutes or ten minutes—he had no sense of time, only pain.

Paul felt himself losing consciousness when suddenly through the headphones his eardrums burst with the sound of screaming babies alternating with deafening acid rock, heavy metal music by Mad Zeppelin and the Ungrateful Dead.

When the two could no longer endure, the mercy of heaven caused them to fall unconscious.

"Okay, guys," the jailer said. "That's enough fun for one night."

The headphones were removed, the battery clamps were undone, and darkness returned to the cell. The door closed as the mirthful voices of the guards faded down the hallway. The entertainment had ended, and now the boredom of the night returned.

The satisfied group of guards settled into their usual routine of sleeping on cots or wherever the marijuana weed they smoked told them to lie down. The jailer dozed off, but only for a short power nap, and he occasionally glanced at the TV monitors that showed the outside of the building, the parking lot and the cell holding areas.

"What ... what's that?" The jailer stirred, blinked, and rubbed his eyes. Straining, he could hear singing from the back holding area.

"Blessed be the name, blessed be the name, blessed be the name of the Lord."

"Shut up, shut up!" a prisoner yelled from another cell.

Paul and Silas could barely hear themselves sing. Their bleeding ears felt on fire and their heads ached, but they wanted to praise God no matter what.

Silas prayed, asking for God to forgive their malefactors. Paul joined in, asking God for victory over the evil that held the city of Philippi. He thanked God for the mercy and forgiveness shown to so many in the streets. He thanked God for the believers who held their faith above the cruelty and persecution they experienced.

With astonishment, the other prisoners heard the sound of prayer and singing issuing from the inner prison. They had been accustomed to hearing shrieks and moans, cursing and swearing. Never before had they heard words of prayer and praise ascending from that gloomy cell. Guards and prisoners marveled and asked themselves who these men could be—who, cold, hungry, and tortured, could yet rejoice.[3]

Most of the guards returned to sleep. One of them got up to

---

[3] Acts of the Apostles, p. 214.

quiet the prisoners. He looked into the holding cell, Paul and Silas were bent over praying.

The guard grunted and returned sleepily to the others. The jailer and his helpers again dozed off to sleep.

In his subconscious, the jailer heard the rumble of a passing truck, a helicopter or an approaching storm, but it got louder and louder. Then the chair he sat on shook violently, as did the floor and walls. Dust and plaster fell from the ceiling, and the AC was torn from the window.

"Earthquake! Earthquake!" He snapped awake along with the other guards.

In terror, the guards fought each other as they raced through the splintered outer door and into the streets to escape the falling debris.

The jailer didn't run. He stood amid a cloud of plaster dust, coughing and shielding his eyes. A strange blinding light streamed from the holding area.

The piercing light penetrated through his fingers and through his eyelids. Within seconds, there was total darkness, quiet, and then whimpering from prisoners.

Never before had the jailer felt such terror. Had the prisoners escaped? Would he pay with his own life for the loss? He trembled because he knew his crime of negligence and dereliction of duty would also cost the lives of his family.

Finding a flashlight, he crept cautiously toward the back area. Ready and tense, his big muscles were prepared for any ambush waiting in the dark.

As he moved slowly, waving the flashlight back and forth, fear took hold of him. Sweat beaded and then dripped profusely over his taut expression. His hands and knees shook uncontrollably.

The door of the missionaries is open! he thought as his worst fears were realized.

From a gapping split in the wall at the end of the corridor, a large hole wide enough for a man to fit through worsened his fears that they were gone. He could see the streetlights outside. *Have the prisoners escaped?*

Shining the flashlight on the floor, he saw the open handcuffs and leg shackles lying in a heap. Panic raced through his mind.

"It's over!" he lamented. "It's over!"

Reaching to his waist holster, he drew his Berretta 9mm pistol, placed the barrel under his chin, paused a moment, and then closed his eyes as his finger curled around the trigger.

"Wait! Wait, my brother!" Paul called from a dark corner. "We are all here. Do not harm to yourself."

The startled jailer dropped the gun from his shaky grip. Upon seeing Paul emerge from the dark cell, he collapsed forward at Paul's feet. His voice was trembling as he pitifully begged, "What must I do to be saved?"

Paul said, "My father in heaven has dispatched an angel from the realm of glory not to free us but to free you. Though you are rough outwardly, He has seen your heart and knows that in His service, you can be the blessing you were born to be."

For a moment Paul saw himself. He remembered his agony, the pounding on the floor for mercy in the Judas Motel. He remembered that moment of surrender.

Tears filled his eyes as he looked at the jailer and remembered the words of His redeemer: "I have loved you with an everlasting love, therefore with loving kindness have I drawn you to Me."

And finally the remembrance that Jesus spoke: "I will never leave you nor forsake you."

"The apostles did not regard their labors in Philippi as in vain. They had met much opposition and persecution, but the intervention of Providence on their behalf, and the conversion of the jailer and his household, more than atoned for the disgrace and suffering they had endured.

The news of their unjust imprisonment and miraculous deliverance became known through that region, and this brought the work of the apostles to the notice of a large number who otherwise would not have been reached.

Paul's labors at Philippi resulted in the establishment of a church whose membership steadily increased. His zeal and devotion, and above all his willingness to suffer for Christ's sake, exerted a deep and lasting influence upon the converts. They prized the precious truths for which the apostles had sacrificed so much, and they gave themselves with wholehearted devotion to the cause of their Redeemer.[4]

[4] Acts of the Apostle, p. 218.

CHAPTER THIRTEEN

I HAVE FOUGHT
A GOOD FIGHT

Paul, Silas, Dr. Luke, and Timothy traveled great distances over the months and years that followed, carrying the good news of hope to those whose lives often seemed hopeless.

Timothy especially matured, being mentored by Paul and Silas. He learned that in his human strength he could not move a real mountain, but through faith and prayer he could move God, who could move the mountain. His mountains were stuttering and in-experience, and by his surrendered life to the Almighty, Timothy became eloquent and seasoned.

Over the years, this energetic and faithful young man received two of Paul's epistles, which appear in the New Testament Bible. From his experience and mentorship, Timothy is thought by some to have penned the book of Hebrews, or certainly under the influence of Paul contributed. Though still no truly known who wrote the book it is rich with hope. The book reflects on the book of Genesis that declares that God the Father, Jesus Christ and the Holy Spirit united in the wonderous creation all things, even this world. The book spoke of Jesus Christ as our compassionate High Priest in the heavenly sanctuary and the famous recitation of heroes of faith.

These all are kept in a special section at the Smithsonian Records Library in Washington, DC.

Mentored by the aged apostle, Timothy endured hardships and relentless test of character and leadership. Never wavering and never losing his sense of mission, he stood firm and focused in his love for God and the early church.

The two friends had become as one in mind and one in purpose for the Gospel. After a time, believers began to call Timothy "Timothy Paul of the tribe of Judah, son of Jacob and son of Paul."

"Paul loved Timothy, as his own son in the faith" (1 Timothy 1:2). The great apostle often drew the younger disciple out, questioning him in regard to scriptural history, and as they traveled from place to place, he carefully taught him how to do successful work.

Paul and Silas, in all their association with Timothy, too sought to deepen the impression that had already been made upon his mind, of the sacred, serious nature of the work of the gospel minister.[5]

As the number of believers grew, so did the animosity toward them. Out of boredom, insanity, or a distraction from the failing Roman economy and Barbarian hordes at Rome's door-step, Emperor Nero contracted a group of arsonists to set fire to Rome. His plan was to blame the Christians and Jews. This would regain his popularity, allow the confiscation of the Jewish wealth, enshrine him as a champion of the gods, and assure him a place among them in the afterlife.

It was amid that great persecution set ablaze by Nero that Paul was arrested on his return to Jerusalem. He was falsely accused by the local high priest and the chief propaganda officer for the temple. He was imprisoned at Caesarea under the governorship of a politician named Festus.

At a quickly arranged trial, Festus heard the augments of the

---

[5] Acts of the Apostles, p. 205.

Jews and knew it was all a sham, but he didn't want to loss favors, like building contracts and kickback money he enjoyed.

When his running buddy from college, King Agrippa, and his wife, Bernice, came to town for a time-share meeting, the conversation turned to the prisoner Paul.

King Agrippa was fascinated and wanted to question Paul himself. He thought, *This could be good for business.*

The next day, Paul stood before King Agrippa. For over an hour, Paul recounted his former life as Agent Saul, his conversion to a follower of Jesus, the forgiveness offered through faith in the Son of God, and the hope and assurance of life eternal in Him.

King Agrippa responded, "Prisoner Paul, you talk a good talk. In fact, you almost made me a believer."

The crowd erupted in laughter.

"But dig this, Paul," Agrippa said, leaning forward. "Catch me later at a more convenient time. I've got stuff to do."

The hearing was over. Paul was escorted out of the court room and back to his imprisonment.

Cupping his hands near the ear of governor Festus, Agrippa whispered, "This guy is okay with me. Let him go."

Festus whispered back, "I would, but he claimed to be a Roman citizen and wants us to send him to Augustus Caesar, at the Senate building in Rome, to hear his case."

"Get out of here, man!" Agrippa was surprised. "He must be out of his mind!"

"Crazy or not, we're flying him to Rome ASAP," Festus said.

Months later, while under house arrest in Rome, Paul wrote in his journal about the flight to Rome.

> I have such a fear of flying and asked if we could go by car or boat, but the guards insisted on flying. I pointed out how the winds this time of year were uncertain and dangerous for flying. They simply

laughed. The pilot standing nearby said, "Don't listen to him. I'm a retired Israel Air Force pilot and know how to fly!"

At first the flight went fine. I was a little nauseated but did not vomit. Then the air bumps increased. The guards looked worried, and I have to admit I was too. The darkness of night came quickly, and rain and lighting batted the airliner up and then down, twisting and turning it with every gust of strong air current. I closed my eyes and prayed.

As I finished praying, my eyes were still closed. I thought I saw an angel at first, and then I realized it was Jesus. He told me not to be afraid. He said I would make it to Rome to testify before the Senate. He warned that all would make it if they stayed on board the plane.

Just then I heard a commotion at the back of the airplane. Some of the crew and a couple of the guards were putting on parachutes.

I called out, "Stop!" Then I told them of my vision. The pilot said he was going to be the first out the plane, but the captain of the guard told him he'd be the first to get a bullet in the head and should stay at the controls.

Needless to say, the storm got worst, and the jet engine on the right wing started to smoke and lose power. The lights in the cabin went out, and luggage was torn from the binds. The yellow oxygen masks daggling from ropes of plastic tubing swung wildly as everybody tried to grab one. Then the plane took a nosedive toward the ground. Below, through openings in the stormy clouds, we could see glimpses of the lights at the Rome airport, but we were in a crash dive. Many on the plane screamed and cried out. I admit my heart was also racing. I prayed, "Lord, you promised to always be with me. Lord, I need You now ... Right now, Father!"

As the airport lights grew larger and the tops of buildings emerged from the clouds, I knew we were moments away from impact. I closed my eyes and simply said, "Jesus."

Having flown before in good weather, I knew we were only a few hundred feet from the runway and were about to crash.

Suddenly the nose of the jet began to lift. I saw the pilot and copilot look at each other as if in surprise while they struggled with the control gears. I heard the flaps extend and then rip off because the speed was too high. The plane shuttered violently, banked right and then left, and was still spiraling downward. Then it lifted.

I remembered hearing stories from the apostles about a time when they were in a storm at sea with Jesus—and how he said, "Peace be still," to the storm and it stopped.

I could feel the plane begin to level off just as the wheels scrapped the runway. A loud explosion sounded when some of the landing gears ripped off along the runway.

The nose of the plane pushed back and forth, trying to get altitude. Before long, the plane settled into a more controlled flight pattern upward. The plane went back out over the Mediterranean Sea to burn off fuel before attempting to land again. The second time, the jet took a more normal glide path with little turbulence. It landed in sparks amid mountains of fire retardant foam sprayed by the numerous fire trucks and emergency vehicles. All were safe, and no one died … as God had promised.

All I could say was, "Thank You, Jesus!" Oh, how my faith was strengthened. I never doubted the promise of Jesus, who said He'd always be with me.

My church family and saints, may the grace and love of our Lord and Savior, Jesus Christ, always fill your hearts.

Signed,

Brother Paul

In those confines, he wrote many letters to the churches spread abroad, and the faith of many grew strong and bold.

In Rome after over a year of waiting for a hearing, the house arrest status was rescinded with all the privileges. It was believed it was at the urging of high Jewish officials, who paid a lot of money to restrict the aging apostle as much as possible.

Paul was transferred and confined to a decrepit dungeon in solitary confinement. Even his writing had to be smuggled out by sympathetic guards. Only a brother, named Omnesipus, was allowed to see him. Most of Paul's friends abandoned him due to the scattering of the believers from the persecution in Rome. Some were arrested, some were sold as slaves, and others made spectacles of sport in the colosseum. A large number were turned into human torches, lighting the way to the arena. Others were mutilated by gladiators, eaten or violated by wild animals in unmentionable ways.

Through the flames and pains of their last moments, the faithful martyrs praised the one who would not forget them, He who one day would raise them victorious.

Paul never forgot his son in the faith, Timothy.

As Timothy opened that final letter from Paul, who was on

death row in the federal prison at Rome, he felt unworthy of the honor God had given him. It was a supreme calling to serve the Lord Jesus and to have God's chosen vessel mentor him.

Holding the treasured letter, Timothy stared at it before reading it. He noticed the torn creases in the aged yellow paper; the large crooked letters from aged hands; wandering diagonal lines; moisture stains of sweat, saliva, or tears; and some misspelled words. It was all so precious to him.

"I have fought a good fight," Timothy reads. "I have finished my course. I have kept the faith."

Timothy's eyes filled with tears as he moved to the end of the letter. The last sentence, "The leather jacket that I left at Troas with Carpus—when you come, Tim, please bring it. I'd like you to bring some of my books too, but most important, please bring my old Bible."

The letter continued, "Timothy, my son, I don't have much time, so please come before the winter. It's cold here. May the Lord Jesus be with you, and may His grace abide with you always. Your father and follow servant in Christ, Paul."

The months melted from winter to spring and then to summer. All appeals had been exhausted with the Roman courts and the Senate. Paul knew one day he must walk the Green Mile, that long strip of green paint that wound along damp corridors, past rusted steel prison doors, and up crumbling cement steps to his execution.

That day came.

Timothy stood, head bowed, at the guard desk. A deep sadness and emptiness exhausted him with a tiredness he had never felt before. His flight was delayed, and the connections rerouted him for hours. He arrived too late to say goodbye. Too late for that last embrace.

"Here!" the guard interrupted his despair and handed Timothy a large dented clothes box. "The old guy, the prisoner—what's his name?" He looked at the tag. "Yeah, Paul. He said to give this to you, and to thank the young man for bringing my jacket. It helped with the cold." The guard released the box and eyed Timothy sympathetically.

Timothy's nose was running. He sniffed, trying to hold the tears, and gave the guard a quick nod of thanks.

Timothy turned slowly to a small room off to the side of the larger package receiving room. He opened the top of the sealed box with a pocketknife and stared. The tears that he tried to hold back found their release in torrents.

There they were, he thought to himself.

The things father Paul prized more than anything else in the world: his black leather jacket, now worn and frayed; the scratched aviators; and, the most precious of all, his Bible.

CHAPTER FOURTEEN

EPILOGUE

According to tradition, Timothy was eventually martyred at Ephesus after standing against the worship of the false pagan god Artemis. From the courage of a life of faithfulness, the example of his hero Paul, and the counsel of the elders, Timothy too was God's champion in the truest sense. Along with Agent Saul, who became God's chosen vessel, they would be heaven's rock stars, along with millions of others bearing crowns heavy with stars of the redeemed.

RG

ACKNOWLEDGEMENTS

Biblical References from the King James Version (KJV) and the New International Version (NIV).

"Acts of the Apostles" by Ellen G. White, Pacific Press Publishing Association.

Agent Saul cover picture used with permission by Dreamtime Stock, Brentwood, Tennessee.

Hand with Crown picture used with permission by Light Stock, Plano, Texas.

Printed in the United States
By Bookmasters